Rainy Day Digest

Want more Rainy Day Writers?
Visit the Rainy Day Writers' website at
https://sites.google.com/site/rainydaywriters2
or use the QR code below.

Rainy Day Digest

RAINY DAY WRITERS
CAMBRIDGE, OHIO

Rainy Day Digest
ISBN-13: 978-1539520535
ISBN-10: 1539520536

Rainy Day Digest. Copyright 2016, CreateSpace. Printed and bound in the United States of America. All rights reserved. No part of this book may be used or reproduced in any manner whatsoever—except by a reviewer who may quote brief passages in a review—without written permission from the publisher.

RAINY DAY WRITERS
CAMBRIDGE, OHIO

Contents

ACKNOWLEDGMENTS
8

EDITOR'S NOTE
9

AGING
12   Please, Not Another Trip
DONNA J. LAKE SHAFER

14   The Ten Most Difficult Things About Being My Age
JOY L. WILBERT ERSKINE

17   The Farewell Address
DONNA J. LAKE SHAFER

EMBARRASSING
20   The Reading of the Passion
BOB LEY

22   OMG
SAMUEL D. BESKET

23   For Want of a Towel
JOY L. WILBERT ERSKINE

24   An Embarrassing Moment
MARTHA F. JAMAIL

26   Sorry, Ladies
SAMUEL D. BESKET

27   Surf's Up
JOY L. WILBERT ERSKINE

29   FIRE! FIRE!
HARRIETTE MCBRIDE ORR

31   What Lights?
SAMUEL D. BESKET

32   The Big Grin
JOY L. WILBERT ERSKINE

34   A Red-faced Incident
DONNA J. LAKE SHAFER

ENTERTAINMENT
37   Test Yourself
BOB LEY

40   Pencils Are Slow
MARTHA F. JAMAIL

43   Ask the Rainy Day Writers
SAMUEL D. BESKET

47   A Little Larceny in All of Us
BOB LEY

FAVORITES
51   8LTRMAX
SAMUEL D. BESKET

53   If I Were a Flower
MARTHA F. JAMAIL

56   Mom's BLT
SAMUEL D. BESKET

58   My Favorite Place
MARTHA F. JAMAIL

HEALTH
61   A Honey of a Cure
BEVERLY WENCEK KERR

64   The Real Skinny on Fat
MARTHA F. JAMAIL

HISTORICAL

67 Orphan on the Tracks
    RICK BOOTH
74 The Duck Pond Disaster of 1896
    RICK BOOTH

FEATURE ARTICLE

78 On Being a Grandfather
    BOB LEY

MENTORING

88 Mentoring
    DONNA J. LAKE SHAFER
90 All-American Work Ethic
    BEVERLY WENCEK KERR
94 A Lesson from Mr. Tom
    SAMUEL D. BESKET
96 The Day I Became an Artist
    MARTHA F. JAMAIL
98 Back Then
    JOY L. WILBERT ERSKINE
101 Prodding from a Friend
    HARRIETTE MCBRIDE ORR
103 The Old Piano Roll Blues
    BEVERLY WENCEK KERR
106 Sister Veronica
    BOB LEY
109 The Person I Would Like to Meet
    MARTHA F. JAMAIL

MILITARY

113 Knittin' for Britain
    DONNA J. LAKE SHAFER
115 Life in the Military
    SAM BESKET
119 One Military Family's Big Adventure
    JOY L. WILBERT ERSKINE
125 The Lucky Ones
    SAMUEL D. BESKET

MISCELLANEOUS

128 A Good Samaritan Surprise
    MARTHA F. JAMAIL
130 Agatha's Mad
    JOY L. WILBERT ERSKINE
132 Think Pink
    DONNA J. LAKE SHAFER
134 Fear…A Delayed Reaction
    MARTHA F. JAMAIL
136 Wishing on a Star
    BEVERLY WENCEK KERR
139 The Bouncers
    JOY L. WILBERT ERSKINE
142 The Break Up
    MARTHA F. JAMAIL

FEATURE ARTICLE

145 Murder & Manhunt
    RICK BOOTH

RETROSPECTIVE

164 Entering the Workforce
HARRIETTE MCBRIDE ORR

168 Prices
BOB LEY

171 It's About Time
DONNA J. LAKE SHAFER

174 Shortcut?
HARRIETTE MCBRIDE ORR

177 Family Life on the Ohio River
BEVERLY WENCEK KERR

180 Sundays
BOB LEY

182 Remember When?
SAMUEL D. BESKET

184 The Thrill of a Lifetime
HARRIETTE MCBRIDE ORR

190 The Lost Art
BOB LEY

193 The Summer of Deep Pond
BEVERLY WENCEK KERR

197 What Am I?
HARRIETTE MCBRIDE ORR

UNBELIEVABLE

199 Desert Dream
BEVERLY WENCEK KERR

203 I Never Believed in Ghosts
DONNA J. LAKE SHAFER

205 Last Dance
MARTHA F. JAMAIL

207 The Ghost of Joe Vargo
SAMUEL D. BESKET

211 Where the Magic Is
JOY L. WILBERT ERSKINE

213 *ALL THE ANSWERS*

214 *ILLUSTRATION CREDITS*

215 *PHOTOGRAPHY CREDITS*

Acknowledgments

Every year, our appreciation grows for all the wonderful folks out there who support the Rainy Day Writers—and the list grows every year. It's impossible to name you all—our readers, our helpers, our sales outlets, our friends. We appreciate every one of you and hope to keep writing the stories and publishing the books you'll want to read for years to come.

Please patronize these businesses, our faithful friends in the Cambridge and Guernsey County area, who provide much-needed assistance and deserve our special recognition:

Crossroads Library
Cambridge Copy Shop
Cambridge News
Cambridge Packaging
Dickens Welcome Center
Michael Neilson Photography
Modern Movements
Mr. Lee's Restaurant
Nothing But Chocolate
Penny Court
Riesbeck's
Shafer Insurance Agency Inc.
Speedy Print
The Daily Jeffersonian

Editor's Note

This year, RDW wanted to try something a little different for our eighth book—some way we could all branch off our usual path, tracking our individual instincts and doing our own thing a little more. I'm betting you'll get to know us each a little better by reading what we write when we're following our hearts.

You may already recognize Rick Booth's forte as historical research, but he also has a knack for digging up oddball tales, recounting them for us in striking comic detail and to maximum effect. Bet you didn't know that about him!

Donna Shafer, Beverly Kerr, and Harriette Orr have gifts that lie in homespun family stories, sometimes even recounted faithfully. Each *has* been known to embellish their memoirs quite liberally, and it's always fun to try to decipher when the tale is true and when they're pulling your leg.

Then there's Sam Besket. His trademark talent resides in stories about his fun-loving youthful ways, experiences in the military, and recollections of working at Champion. He's got the gift of gab and is, to be truthful, happier regaling us with a story than writing it. Those of us who know him know Sam's never outgrown having fun and getting in trouble.

Bob Ley and Martha Jamail, the talented artists who graciously illustrated this book, are, in real life, the RDW "cohorts in Catholic crime." Whether written or spoken, their stories are what I would call "classy," but satisfyingly tinged with parochial school shenanigans. You'll discover their readers are left with a delightful sense of the good in the world.

That leaves me. I would let you figure me out for yourself, but Sam won't let me get by with that. Here's what he says you ought to know about me: "Joy Erskine was raised an Air Force brat. She carries the discipline and can-do attitude she grew up with in the military into civilian life. It's widely suspected in RDW that in her secret life she serves our country as an undercover operative for the C.I.A."

And if you believe that, you might just be a candidate for the funny farm—or induction into the Rainy Day Writers.

–Joy L. Wilbert Erskine, Editor

AGING

ag•ing (ā′jĭng) *n.* **1.** The process of growing old or maturing. **2.** A process for imparting the properties of age. *Syn.* Declining, waning, falling, sinking, mellowing, getting on or along, maturing, senescent, developing, fermenting, wasting away, wearing out, growing old, lapsing, outworn, fading, crumbling, slumping; *all* (D): one foot in the grave, on the downgrade, stale.

Please, Not Another Trip

BY DONNA J. LAKE SHAFER

Endless horizons for the modern traveler.

During a lifetime, it sometimes comes to one's attention that she can no longer do many of the things she once loved to do, like travel to distant places. But now, thanks to family, extended family, and social media, she can tag along.

During the past year or so, I have journeyed to Montana several times for heartbreaking visits. There was a family cruise to the Caribbean, where we visited interesting seaports and enjoyed activities aboard ship. There was a visit to southern California in August and I was right there for the surprise gathering to celebrate the "big six-oh" birthday of a son.

Several weeks were spent in "the big city," where a couple young ballerinas studied with the American School of Ballet. Later, it was off to Peru to visit relatives.

A sentimental, heart-wrenching trip was made to India for the funeral ceremony of a loved one and to visit extended family throughout parts of that country. Other family members visited several countries of South America and later were off to

Vietnam, Cambodia, and Japan.

Belgium, where I had visited a few years ago, was on the agenda for others. It was wonderful walking the cobbled streets and seeing the outdoor vendors and eateries again. Fortunately, I was visiting English-speaking relatives my first time there, as my French was practically nonexistent. And while we're in Europe, let's not forget Austria, my first time in that beautiful land in the Alps.

A couple trips to Hawaii by different family members were most welcome. There I enjoyed the many attributes of those lovely islands.

Happily, some family members came from the Atlanta area to visit us. One group made their return trip by way of Columbus, Ohio. It seems that the daddy of the family wanted to see for himself (are you ready for this?) "The House That Harley Built." That's right, he wanted to see the stadium at Ohio State University. The poor boy's education had been sadly neglected and he had never seen it except through television, so the trip there was an absolute must.

As you can see, thanks to the generosity of loved ones, I have been given the opportunity to visit places that, at this time, would be otherwise impossible.

So I'm enjoying life vicariously these days, but hoping the travels this year are a little less intense. Quite frankly, Dear Readers, I'm exhausted.

What? Me, worry?

I drive way too fast to worry about cholesterol.

The Ten Most Difficult Things about Being My Age

BY JOY L. WILBERT ERSKINE

That difficult stage, somewhere between raising kids and courting mortality.

It's not that I'm all that old. Really, it isn't. It's just that I'm not that young anymore either. When you think about it, there are difficult things about any age. I've been around long enough to know that, but since I'm finding today's challenges particularly vexing, let me count down my Top 10 Challenges of being the age I am now. I think you may be able to relate.

Challenge #10:

My kids don't need my help any more. That's the good news. The bad news is my husband and parents already do, and he and I live here and they live two states away. Makes life a little too interesting at times. And I'd really like to know how I managed to miss out on the middle, "enjoying retirement," part that's supposed to be there between generations.

Challenge #9:

Trying to see through cheaters to trim my toenails. It doesn't help that I have to work around a bad hip and a few extra pounds. No matter how I go at it, my toes are just a little too close for my distance vision to work, and a little too far for reading glasses. That's the one downside of having cataracts removed, I suppose. Maybe if I quit drinking milk and back off on the calcium supplements my toenails won't grow so fast.

Challenge #8:

Living on a limited income and watching the price of food and medication skyrocket, wondering if Social Security is still going to be there when I get old enough. Or will I *ever* get old enough? I feel *dang* old enough.

Challenge #7:

Watching young, slim joggers with earbuds race by me like they need the exercise, while I puff around Northwood Cemetery knowing it's never going to help me lose any weight. I just try to keep moving, reading gravestones as I go for entertainment. And now that I think of it, I sure do know a lot of the folks in residence up there. Kind of a grim reminder. Maybe I better try walking in Cambridge City Park.

Challenge #6:

Give me just one good reason I should stay on Facebook. All I wanted was a way to stay in touch with the grandkids, who have moved on to other things I can't begin to keep up with, like Twitter, Instagram, Tumblr, Snapchat, Kik, Vine, and whatever the heck else they do that I probably don't want to know about. What I got with Facebook was a black hole that can suck me in for hours, till I'm accomplishing nothing. But I have to check back in, just in case the grandkids have been there and I missed them. Oh, for the old days…

Challenge #5:

Just trying to keep my computer running and internet up, when all I want to do is sit down and check my email, do a little research, and knock out a couple stories without the aggravation. So much to ask, I know. There's something inordinately wrong about being on a phone-voice-recognition level with your computer guy and internet provider. "Hi Justin! Hi Pete! Yep, same time, same place. See you shortly." Just call us the "Lunch Bunch"—Justin, Pete, and me, we go way back.

Challenge #4:

Tracing my genealogy back to my 6th great-grandparents and then finding out the family line's been hacked and not all those family members are mine after all. I should know better—it's all I can do to keep track of the grandkids, after all.

Challenge #3:

Mundane tasks take up most of the day. I hate repeat tasks like making beds, fixing meals, brushing teeth, taking showers, napping, and going to the bathroom. By the time all that is done, it's time to start over. And I sure wish I didn't have to spend so much time sleeping. What a waste of perfectly good time! I think once you've done it, it ought to stay done. With all that repetitive nonsense, how am I supposed to get to the fun stuff?

Challenge #2:

I've got a quilt I've been "working on" for the last ten years. It gets relegated to the "after the other stuff I need to do" list. I'll probably get it done just in time to "sleep" under it in my casket. (Hmmm, so, maybe I shouldn't be in such a hurry to finish.)

And (drumroll please…)

Challenge #1:

The #1 challenge of being the age I am now is…knowing all that I know, with no one around who has any intention of listening.

Guess that's why I write.

The Farewell Address

BY DONNA J. LAKE SHAFER

Life's little lessons: The benefits of planning ahead.

The patriarch of the Simpson family, Robert T., pushed himself back from the remains of a sumptuous Thanksgiving dinner. Dabbing his chin with a linen napkin, he slowly glanced around the table, briefly studying his guests.

They were fourteen in all; two sons and their wives, daughter Jennifer and her husband Charlie, plus six teenaged grandchildren.

Looking first to Nancy, his wife, and then each of his children in turn, Bob addressed them.

"Your mother and I, after much discussion and not a little soul searching, have made a decision which affects you all. Since we're here together, I've chosen this time to advise you that we have sold the business."

"What do you mean?" Bob Jr. yelled, spitting out a mouthful of coffee.

"I mean," replied his dad. "I've sold the business."

"But you can't," screamed his son, David.

"Oh, but I can," proclaimed his father icily. "I can, and I did."

"What about us?" asked Charlie plaintively.

"Well, here's the deal. Your mother and I own seventy percent of the stock in the company. You three collectively own the remainder. In an agreement with the new owners, you boys may stay on at your present salaries for six months. At that time, they and you will decide whether you stay or not. You've all received generous paychecks, bonuses, and dividends during the years. I doubt if you've saved much, if any, judging from the way you live, and you certainly haven't worked much, unless you call recreational golfing work."

Ignoring the cries of protest heard about the room, Robert went on. "Anyway, you're on your own. Oh, and don't count on inherited wealth from us. There won't be much, as we intend to donate generously to our favorite charities. As for Mother and me, we plan to enjoy the fruits of our labors. While we're young enough and healthy enough, we'll be doing some traveling. Next week, we're going on a cruise, for starters.

"Oh, by the way, we hope you enjoyed your last meal in this house. It's been sold and we'll be moving out to a little place in the Valley."

The Thanksgiving observance ended soon after this announcement. As the Simpson's dazed guests were leaving, Robert called out, "Oh, one more thing. We'll be gone for a few months, so Merry Christmas to all and to all, a good night."

Food for thought

The early bird might get the worm, but the second mouse gets the cheese.

EMBARRASSING

em•bar•rass•ing (ĕm-băr'əs-ĭng) *v.* **1.** Making (someone) feel confused and foolish in front of other people. Tr.v. **1.** Placing in doubt, perplexity, or difficulties. **b.** Involving in financial difficulties **c.** Causing to experience a state of self-conscious distress. **2.** Hampering the movement of. **b.** hinder, impede. **3.** Making intricate or complicated. *Int. v.* Becoming anxiously self-conscious. *adj.* **em•bar•rass•able** \-ə-sə-bəl *Syn:* difficult, disturbing, confusing, distracting, bewildering, puzzling, rattling, perplexing, delicate, distressing, disconcerting, upsetting, discomforting, ticklish, flustering, troubling, troublesome, worrisome, uncomfortable, awkward, disagreeable, inopportune, helpless, unseemly, uneasy, mortifying, shameful, annoying, inconvenient, sticky.

The Reading of the Passion

BY BOB LEY

A draining dramatic debut.

Palm Sunday. That meant the reading of the Passion at Sunday Mass—a long reading depicting the death of Jesus.

Traditionally, young men from our fourth grade class would vie to read the various parts of this Gospel from the altar, making it more like a play. The nuns considered it an honor and most of us were volunteered. Nuns had real power. Several of us tried out for the roles. Our teacher, Sister Mary Leah, told us she would announce her selections at three o'clock. Nuns can also be melodramatic.

The tension and excitement built throughout the afternoon, with all of us putting on an air of studied nonchalance. The clock hit three and the dismissal bell sounded. The boys from whom she would make her selection gathered dutifully in the hall near her room. Sister appeared with her clipboard in hand, signifying her earnestness in choosing.

She began announcing her choices. One by one, the roles were assigned with no less importance than an Oscar. (I told you some nuns had a flair for the melodramatic!) The last role, that of Jesus, and by far the most coveted, was left until last. There were four of us left for the one role. "One of you will do Jesus. The rest are dismissed." With that she gave the role to me and announced that there would be two weeks of rigorous after school rehearsals. The last three told me, to a man, they were pleased not to have to go through all that! I was inclined to agree with them.

She was right. It was rigorous and it was two weeks. Each of us had our role down to the last inflection, along with a few lessons in stagecraft.

Palm Sunday arrived. We met in the altar boys' sacristy, a small room off the altar, and donned floor length black cassocks. With our hair Brylcreemed to perfection, faces scrubbed pink, and nerves ratcheted to the limit, we were ready!

Father Murphy gave us the signal and we all solemnly stepped out and positioned ourselves in front of each microphone. The reading began. Part of our rehearsal included memorizing enough of what we read to allow time to look at the audience. "Making eye contact," Sister had intoned.

My first lines came up and I began. Remembering to look out at the congregation, who of course were not there when we practiced, I saw four hundred faces looking at me.

I froze and, within seconds, realized I had wet my pants. Nervously glancing down, I was relieved to find the cassock had covered my indiscretion. When I finished my part, while checking the floor for a tell-tale puddle, I thankfully did not see one. However, I felt my shoes would probably gurgle as I left the altar.

We finished and walked back to the sacristy, with me in quick march leading the parade. I made some excuse about not hanging around for the reflected glory of our parents and got to the car as quickly as possible.

I was the only one who knew what happened that day, but I can assure you, after being "Jesus" it was humbling.

OMG

BY SAMUEL D. BESKET

On overtime overload.

Working seven days a week is a grind. After several months, your days and weeks blend together. Unfortunately, sometimes it is necessary.

One sunny July day, our office manager called me to the front office. On arrival, I was greeted by a large basket of flowers and balloons.

"These are for you," she said.

"Can't be," I replied. "It's not Father's Day or my birthday."

"Just read the card."

As soon as I saw the "Happy Anniversary" on the front of the card, a cold chill ran down my back. *OMG, I forgot our anniversary.* Stunned, I was unable to speak. My first thought was to call a local florist and have them send my wife two dozen peach roses.

It was then I realized my wife was standing behind me.

By this time, half the front office was watching. We all had a good laugh, including my wife, who knew what it was like to work seven days a week.

For Want of a Towel

BY JOY L. WILBERT ERSKINE

The perils of sibling impropriety.

As the oldest child, I was sometimes enlisted to care for my younger siblings. One warm summer evening, my little sister and I were upstairs taking a bath while Mom visited outside with a neighbor. Despite my best efforts at entertaining her, Janny just wouldn't stay in the tub. Slick as soapsuds, she slipped away from me altogether, scampering down the stairs and out the back door wearing nothing but bare skin.

Anxious to follow my mother's instructions to take care of the little imp, I gave chase, pausing only momentarily to wrap myself with a towel. Sprinting outside to Mom, I dramatically vented my frustration about the difficulty of corralling my cute, but doggedly determined little charge.

"And now she's out here running around naked! I don't know what to do. She just won't listen."

Immediately recognizing the unwarranted distress in my plea, Mom advised me not to worry. Janny was a toddler; it would be all right. Then, with a pointed glance at my little towel, she added calmly, "but you might want to consider a little less exposure yourself, Joy."

An Embarrassing Moment

BY MARTHA F. JAMAIL

Keeping it all in the family.

It was just an ordinary Saturday morning when our air conditioner stopped working. My husband made a call and, before leaving to run errands, told me a repairman would come in the afternoon around one o'clock.

At 10 a.m., I decided I'd have enough time to color my hair, so I applied the solution. Knowing I had a ten-minute wait time before rinsing, I also applied Nair hair removal cream on my upper lip. After only five minutes had passed, the doorbell rang. I panicked, knowing it wouldn't be my husband. Looking in the mirror, I saw the reflection of a woman with her entire head plastered with black goo and a mustache of white cream!

There was nothing I could do. I thought quickly about wrapping a towel around my head, turban-like, but that would certainly ruin a good towel, and the cream on my face was just beginning to work and would take too much time to adequately remove before I needed to answer the door.

I approached slowly, hoping it was my neighbor, Patty, but no, it was the air conditioning repairman, and he was quite young. I just knew the poor guy would be scared out of his wits!

So...I took a deep breath, opened the door slightly, and said, "I'm going to open the door, but I don't want to startle you. I'm coloring my hair and I have cream on my face, so be prepared."

As I opened the door all the way, the young man looked at me and laughed, saying, "You don't have to worry, Ma'am. You look just like my mother!"

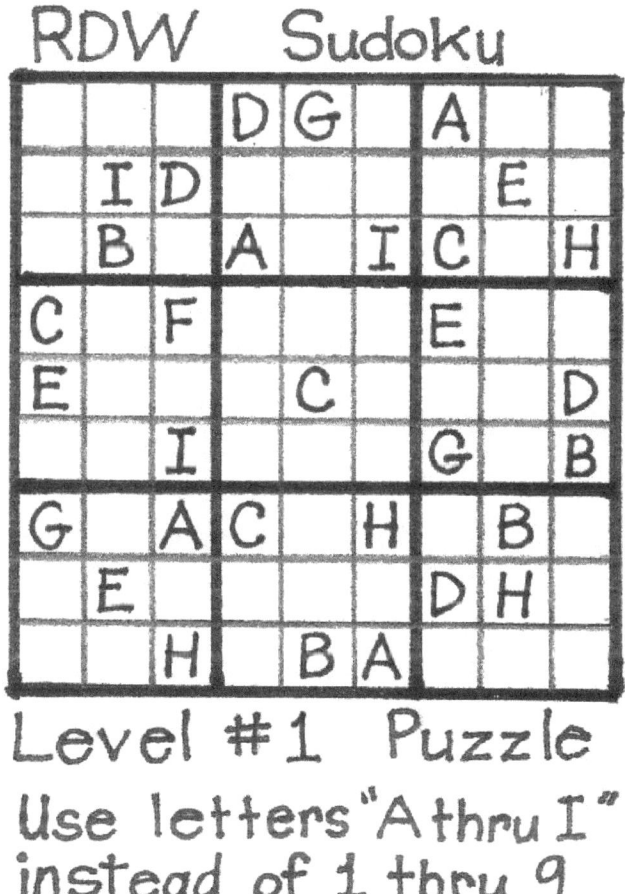

RDW Sudoku

Level #1 Puzzle

Use letters "A thru I" instead of 1 thru 9

Solution on page 213.

Sorry, Ladies

BY SAMUEL D. BESKET

A case of mistaken identity.

 I love to travel; unfortunately, my bowels sometimes interrupt my vacation schedule. Maybe I'm too used to operating on schedules and my innards get confused when I'm away from home.

Such was my predicament during one of our visits out West. We were in a large superstore when I realized I needed a bathroom quickly. A lady pointed to a large restroom sign at the far end of the store. Everything in me urged me to proceed with all dispatch. Arriving, I entered the first door I saw.

A few minutes later, to my horror, I heard ladies talking. I realized, in my haste to satisfy the demands of nature, I had entered the ladies restroom.

Finally, after a few minutes of trying to figure out what to do, I straightened my clothes, opened the door, smiled at the ladies and left. Needless to say, that was my last visit to that store.

Surf's Up!

BY JOY L. WILBERT ERSKINE

Fit to be tide.

Whenever we visited my grandparents in California, we looked forward to a trip to Oceanside to visit relatives and spend a day at the beach. We looked every bit the tourist as we skipped excitedly the block or two to the sand in our flip-flops and swimsuits, carrying towels and sunscreen. Seagulls sailed overhead, squawking, eyeballing our picnic lunch. We habitually settled our gear in a sunny spot near the fishing pier and took the time to walk it to the end, checking out the vendors and bait sellers and watching fishermen bring in interesting sea creatures.

But I could hardly wait to get into the water. I loved the sensation of the ocean scooping the sand from under my feet, lifting me up, and propelling me powerfully back to the shoreline. The seawater smelled fishy and sand kept washing into my bikini bottoms, but I wanted to ride the surf all day. Wading far out into the deep until the tips of my toes barely skimmed the ocean floor and the rhythmic rise and fall of the water left me a little out of control, I'd lift my feet and let the rolling tide transport me back to land.

Over and over, the breakers deposited me on the shell-strewn shore, dripping, salty, and happy. It was an idyllic day…until I stood to wave to my mom and realized my swimsuit top was floating back out with the tide.

Water sense of humor!

What did the Pacific Ocean say to the Atlantic Ocean?...Nothing, it just waved.

Did you hear about the red ship that collided with the blue ship?...All the sailors were marooned.

Why are there fish at the bottom of the sea?...Because they dropped out of school.

What's the best way to communicate with a fish?...Drop it a line!

If the earth was flat and a fish swam over the edge, where would it go?...Trouter space.

What did the magician say to the fisherman?...Pick a cod, any cod!

FIRE! FIRE!

BY HARRIETTE MCBRIDE ORR

The old push mower is looking pretty good about now.

OMG! The smoke has alerted the neighbors and everyone is running this way.

I was just mowing the lawn and had to add more gas to the mower. As I pulled the rope to restart it, I saw a trickle of gasoline running down from the lid. Immediately, it caught fire. I hightailed it out of there, lickety split. *VAVOOM!* went the fuel tank and black smoke and flames shot into the air.

Now I hear sirens. Someone has called the fire department! I can hear them all the way out Eighth Street and then, as they turn up Wall Avenue, the noise gets louder. Neighbors are running out to wave them down.

With a last blast of the siren, the big red fire truck comes to a screeching stop in front of our house. The firemen jump off the truck and head on a run for the side yard.

Having lived in the country all my life, I can't believe all this commotion over a burning lawnmower, now just a smoldering piece of junk, being sprayed with fire extinguishers.

I want to run and hide but it's too late for that.

Spying the empty gas can nearby, the chief said, "Bet

you put gas into a hot mower, didn't you?"

I nodded my head yes.

"You just don't know how lucky you are not to have been burned. Hope you learned a lesson here. You just don't pour gasoline into a hot mower, young lady."

I hung my head and sniffled an "I won't do it again, ever!"

Never, ever, did I start a lawnmower after that without watching for it to blow up. Lesson learned and not forgotten.

Not too speedy

An elderly, well-dressed woman left the department store in Pleasanton with her arms loaded with packages. Running footsteps alerted her that something wasn't quite right, but two young men approached before she could react.

Grabbing the purse from her shoulder, one of them shouted, "Now we've got money for our drugs," as their buddy picked them up in his car and they sped out of the parking lot.

The good news is that they were busted. They used her credit card to purchase gas at Speedway. To make capture even easier, one of the robbers used his Speedy Rewards card. Guess he wanted to make sure he received his reward points.

Yep! Can't make that stuff up.

What Lights?

BY SAMUEL D. BESKET

Directionally challenged, maybe?

I never get lost when I travel; I'm just sometimes not where I want to go. So it was as we drove through a small southern Tennessee town. I remarked how modern the town was. They had buried all the utility services, so the street was devoid of the ugly lines and cables we see so often paralleling streets.

Apparently, they were very friendly people too, since several of them were waving at us.

It was then my wife remarked, "You do know the traffic signals are on the side of the street, don't you?"

This timely remark probably saved an accident as I spied a traffic signal off to my right that had just turned red.

Fortunately, above the signal pole was an interstate highway sign that pointed us in the direction we needed to go.

The Big Grin

BY JOY L. WILBERT ERSKINE

An evening of brotherly love.

There are three things she told me never to do. One: Don't fight with your brother. Two: Don't wear your underwear twice without washing. And three: Don't say anything if you can't say something good. Mother was always right.

I was 17, dating Charles. Smitten, I looked forward to every moment with him, so I convinced Mother to invite him to dinner. That evening Daddy led us to the table, seating Charles across from me and my brother, John.

All was going well when my brother suddenly turned Cheshire cat. I brushed him off, muttering, "Stop it, stupid." His toothless 7-year-old grin never wavered. Mother and Daddy were focused on Charles, who looked my way between bits of conversation, otherwise reserving his attention for my parents, who queried him mercilessly.

Slipping my smiling sibling the evil eye, I returned to the conversation just as John pinched my underarm with fingertips like vice grips. Eyes welling, I managed a smile, disguising my pain as Charles' perplexed gaze fell upon me. Brother John giggled under his breath. I might have killed him, but turned my attention willfully to my plate. Bite by bite, I strived for control, John all the while grinning in his own little Wonderland.

Turning discreetly, I planted a sharp kick on his… chair. Shock waves raced up my leg, knocking me and my chair to the floor. Feet flailing, skirts over my head, I realized Charles had an unprecedented view of my, yes, you guessed it, unwashed knickers. Stunned, he gasped as Mother leapt to my rescue.

Mortified, I glared at John, a reflex explanation escaping my lips: "Damn that cat!" Charles' face went white. My parents turned purple. Punishment was swift: mouth washing, apologies, and a month's restriction. Charles never called again. And Brother John is still grinning.

Classic advice from Mom

"Make sure you always have your own money."
"Modesty is beyond reproach."
"You can do anything with clean hands, clean teeth, and an empty bladder!"
"Use milk to get ink stains out of clothing."
"Never call a man unless you're already in a relationship—men are hunters, not gatherers."
"Mind your manners!"
"Be kind and love your sisters. After your father and I are gone, you will need each other."
"This, too, shall pass."
"Look in the mirror and see if you see a friend in there. If you don't, take a longer look and get the friend back."
"Because I said so!"
"Soap is cheap—there's no excuse for being dirty!"
"Ask your father!"

A Red-faced Incident

BY DONNA J. LAKE SHAFER

Leave it to a guy to screw up a perfectly lovely evening.

 Talk about embarrassing moments. It would take some time to live this one down.

It was Julie's practice when introducing a new garment to her wardrobe to wash it when possible, or dry-clean when not, before wearing. After all, many hands had handled it during the creating process and one can't be too careful.

Julie had learned through the years to take good care of her clothes. As a child many were hand-me-downs so had already seen some wear. It was her habit to turn hangers to the back of the closet unless the clothing was not quite fresh, in which case it was hung in the opposite direction, facing the front, and carefully checked over before wearing again.

The outing was somewhat impromptu. It was a lazy afternoon when her "beloved" suggested they take in a movie, then have an early dinner at their favorite restaurant. It sounded like a plan, so she quickly checked out films and show times on the computer and learned that they'd have to hurry to make a matinee.

Dashing to her closet, Julie grabbed a pair of jeans and a warm sweater and dressed quickly. She applied makeup, hurriedly combed her hair, and slipped on some shoes. Inspecting her image in the full-length mirror, she proclaimed to herself, "Well, that's as good as its going to get," and out they went.

The pair made it into the theater just as the lights dimmed and they were able to enjoy a rather amusing two hours of film.

Later, Julie and her escort entered the restaurant of their choice, where they chanced to greet a party of eight old friends who were already seated and celebrating a birthday. There were happy greetings all around. As Julie leaned forward to greet the hostess, she felt something nudge her backside. Turning to see what was happening, her spouse's hand was immediately in front of her face. He was waving a long narrow strip of plastic listing information concerning her new, apparently unwashed, jeans. He called out for all to hear, "What's this? It was stuck on your pants."

"Oh, jeez!" she answered, quickly grabbing the offending thing from his hands. "Give me that!"

Amid gales of laughter from the birthday celebrating group, a red-faced Julie and her bewildered spouse quickly removed themselves from the scene and were soon seated by the hostess. Menus were presented and orders taken.

The couple very quietly enjoyed the remainder of the evening. Sort of.

This, I gotta see...

The only substitute for good manners is fast reflexes.

ENTERTAINMENT

en•ter•tain•ment (ən'**tər-tān**'mənt) *n.* **1.** The act of entertaining. **2.** The art or field of entertaining. **3.** Something that amuses, pleases, or diverts, esp. a performance or show. **4.** The pleasure afforded by being entertained; amusement. **5.** *Archaic* Maintenance; support. **6.** *Obsolete* Employment. *Syn:* amusement, enjoyment, merriment, bodily enjoyment, divertissement (French), fun, pleasure, delight, cheer, sport, play, recreation, frolic, pastime, diversion, recreation, relaxation, distraction.

Test Yourself

BY BOB LEY

See how many of these common words for which you can find the correct definition.

1. **PORTEND:** a) make believe, act out; b) act as a bartender; c) foretell; d) to care for badly.
2. **ANTIPASTO:** a) before the meal; b) hating spaghetti; c) against using glue; d) your mother's sister.
3. **ACCUSTOMED:** a) brought over the Mexican border; b) familiarized; c) Halloween outfit; d) blamed.
4. **IMPAIRED:** a) put into groups of two; b) small child breathing; c) diminished; d) blind date.
5. **PREDOMINATELY:** a) the stronger element, b) setting up dominoes; c) early beating; d) not a word.
6. **STATEMENT:** a) intended for Ohio; b) one of 50 state candies; c) whispered; d) announcement, proclamation.
7. **OUTBREAK:** a) an eruption; b) the right side of first base; c) fracture that pierces skin; d) exterior wall crack.
8. **LEAD: a)** a very heavy metal; b) pulled by a rope or leash; c) first in a parade; d) all the above.
9. **BENEVOLENT:** a) was a strong force; b) kind and compassionate; c) a movie star; d) Ben during a fight.
10. **PENINSULA:** a) a high priced writing instrument; b) fiberglass around a pigpen; c) neck

of land; d) a dancer's outfit.
11. **INCIDENT:** a) dental insurance; b) putting a tooth in; c) an occurrence, a happening; d) frightening experience.
12. **DIRECTORY:** a) Mapquest, for example; b) satellite TV company; c) a true tale; d) register, index.
13. **NINTY:** a) less than 91; b) more than 89; c) halfway between 85 and 95; d) ninety misspelled.
14. **REIMBURSEMENT:** a) another purse; b) pay double for something; c) repayment; d) a plumbing term.
15. **OUTLANDISH:** a) an island; b) absurd; c) a serving of foreign food; d) wooden restroom shed.
16. **MOONSTRUCK:** a) silly/foolish because of love; b) hit by an asteroid; c) obscene gesture; d) vehicle belonging to Mr. Moon.
17. **PANHANDLE:** a) to beg for money; b) used to hold a pot; c) across the handle; d) restock a kitchen.
18. **BOA CONSTRICTOR:** a) a too-tight feather scarf; b) a builder of boas; c) large reptile; d) the drain in a watercraft hull.
19. **STEVEDORE:** a) the opening to Steve's house; b) his boat; c) waterfront manual laborer; d) Steve in love.
20. **ANTIDISESTAB-LISHMENT-ARIANISM:** This is a free one, folks. Considered the longest word in the dictionary, it means "opposition to state support of a particular religion."

How did you fare? Here's how to tell: 16-20 correct—Genius; 12-15 correct—Very Good; Less than 11—Think about joining Rainy Day Writers! Answers on page 213.

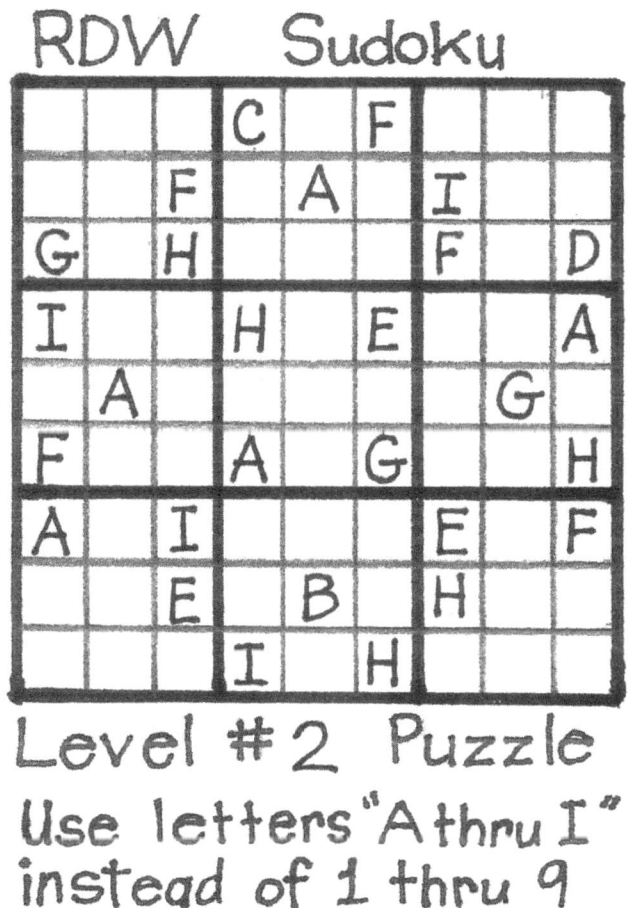

Solution on page 213.

Pencils Are Slow

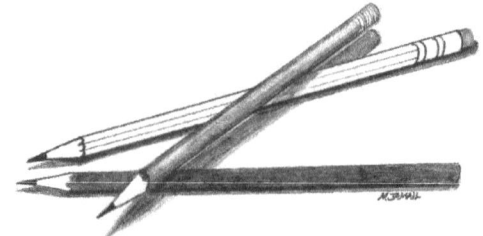

BY MARTHA F. JAMAIL

Pencil me in, please...

Actually, I don't think pencils are slow. Natalie Goldberg does. She is the author of one of the best books on writing I have come across. The title is "Writing Down the Bones," taken from an article in the Writer's Digest.

I read Natalie's book from cover to cover on the first day, stopping only to complete a couple of exercises that she recommended. (She's very persuasive.) Now, back to the pencils, she said that pencils were slow and had drag as you composed your piece on paper. Ball point pens were just as bad, so she highly recommended that a writer invest in a nice Sheaffer pen—the kind with an ink cartridge. Not only would it make your writing flow, but the pen would write so elegantly that every word would seem as important as the flowery writing of the Declaration of Independence.

Her next recommendation was the type of paper you wrote on. Her choice was a spiral composition book. The cheap kind you can get for 25 cents at the back to school sales. Why? Because the paper is so inexpensive, you feel free to express yourself easily. She had filled so many of them with her writing, she said they could form a five foot wall.

Writing, she said, should be done every day for at least 10 minutes, whether or not you have anything important to say. There should be no editing, correcting, or rephrasing at this stage of writing. You are only to release your thoughts on paper. (I have to confess that my first exercise in writing—the 10-minute exercise—was in defense of the maligned pencil.) As an artist, I have great respect for all pencils, from the lowly yellow school pencil to the Venus drawing pencils used to create black and white drawings. Cheap pencils are just as handy and available as 25 cent spiral notebooks, so my first piece of timed writing was done with a cheap pencil on a yellow legal size notepad. That's all I had at the time.

Maybe I should purchase a Sheaffer pen, or would a Sharpie fine point marker work just as well? My grocery list is written with a Sharpie and the writing does flow. But no matter what I choose, Natalie Goldberg has done a number on me. My legal pad is full, even if it was written in pencil, and I now have many new ideas for writing topics. Some of her suggestions are listed below:

1. Begin with "I remember…" and don't be concerned if it was 5 seconds ago or 5 years ago.
2. Take something you feel strongly about, whether it is positive or negative, and write about it as if you love it. Then flip over and write about the same thing as if you hate it.
3. Choose a color—for instance, blue—and take a 15-minute walk. On your walk, notice wherever there is blue. Come back to your notebook and write for 15 minutes.
4. Visualize a place you really love. Be there,

and see the details. Then write about it. It could be the corner of your bedroom, an old tree you sat under one summer, a table at your favorite restaurant, or a place on a beach. What colors are there...sounds...
5. smells? When someone else reads it, they should know how much you love to be there. Not just by saying you love it, but how you write the details.
6. Write about losing a loved one.
7. What is your first memory?
8. Write about the streets of your city.
9. Describe a grandparent.
10. Write about swimming--the stars--being most frightened—green places—the closest you ever felt to God or nature—reading and books that have changed your life—physical endurance—a teacher you had—DON'T BE ABSTRACT—write the real stuff. Be honest and be detailed.
10. Continue to generate your own writing material and topics.

If you enjoy writing, or just want to try, you could buy a Sheaffer pen, but please feel free to use the lowly pencil if that's all you have around. It's what you write that's most important. I also highly recommend you read Natalie Goldberg's book.

"Lead"ing question

If the #2 pencil is the most popular, why is it still #2?

ASK the Rainy Day Writers

Disclaimer: The Rainy Day Writers accept no responsibility for advice gone awry. Heed this counsel at your own risk.

Dear RDW:
My girlfriend is hot and pretty, but a lousy cook. Should I overlook the cooking and ask her to marry me?

—**Jessie in Buffalo.**

Dear Jessie:
The question is do you want to satisfy your eyes, or your stomach? If it's your eyes, I hope you don't mind eating Big Macs for the next thirty years and dying of a heart attack at age fifty. My advice would be to go with a gal who makes a great pot roast.

—**Sam from RDW**

* * * * *

Dear RDW:
I'm 50, divorced, raised three kids, and have a great job. Now it's my time. I'm currently dating a guy eight years younger than me. He's good looking, has six-pack abs, and is a great lover. My concern is he only works part time at the library and lives with his mother. He has asked me to marry him. Should I accept?

—**Confused in Cambridge**

Dear Confused:
If I told you not to marry him would you listen? I thought you said you raised three children. Why do you want to co-mother another? My advice is to look for a guy who owns a string of restaurants and has a yacht on Lake Erie. You'll never have to cook again and you'll get a great tan on the water.
—**Joy from RDW**

* * * * *

Dear RDW:
My husband always gets lost when we're on vacation. He refuses to use a road map or the GPS app on his smart phone. Any advice on how to get him to change?
—**Lost in Lore City**

Dear Lost:
First of all, you have to understand the way a man's mind works. It goes against everything they were taught since Biblical times to ask for directions; it's what they do. Now you know why Moses wandered in the desert for forty years. Just sit back and consider every trip an adventure.
—**Martha from RDW**

* * * * *

Dear RDW:
My grandkids seldom visit me and fail to acknowledge any gifts I send them. I have dropped several hints, but nothing seems to work. Any advice on how I can get them to respond to my gifts and visit me?
—**Lonesome in Byesville**

Dear Lonesome:
Take it from someone who has been around since Harry Truman was in knickers. You have to "fight fire with fire." I would cut off the gifts, but send them an unsigned check. When they call, tell

them you will sign the check when they visit. Then use them for free tech support when they arrive.

*—***Max from RDW**

* * * * *

Dear RDW:
Twice a year my husband sends me to the local Ford dealership to get the air changed in the tires of our cars. He claims the air gets stale and, just like your engine oil, needs changed every five thousand miles. The mechanics gladly do this for me, but snicker behind my back. Does air grow stale in car tires?
—**Looking Silly in Senecaville**

Dear Looking:
This answer is easy. The only stale air is between your hubby's ears.

P.S. I would keep him away from the family checkbook too. —**Bob from RDW**

* * * * *

Dear RDW:
I've spent the last twenty years working so my twin boys could get a good education. Both have finished college and moved back home. Now instead of looking for a job, they just lay around the house all day playing video games and waiting on me to come home from work to fix supper. They say they are trying to "find" themselves. How can I motivate them to go look for a job?
—**Motivated Mom in Old Washington**

Dear Motivated:
You have to understand, men are like dogs. As long as you feed them, they won't leave. I would give them a deadline. Tell them if they

don't find a job in thirty days, they will find themselves at the Y.M.C.A.
   —**Harriet from RDW**

* * * * *

Dear RDW:
My 90-year-old father has a lot of money. He has been chasing a 22-year-old neighbor. I warned him that an affair might be hard on the heart. He said, "If she dies, she dies." Should I be worried?
 —**Concerned Daughter in Kipling**

Dear Concerned:
Are you concerned about your dad, the neighbor, or yourself? Let your dad enjoy himself. After all, at ninety he doesn't have many years left. Have your dad donate his wealth to charity, then

check out the neighbor to see if she is still interested.
   —**Bev from RDW**

* * * * *

Dear RDW:
My wife of thirty years and I argue a lot. No matter what I say, she always has to have the last word. How can I get my way and have the last word? —**Last Word in Quaker City**

Dear Last:
My friend John from the hardware store has the answer to this. According to John, if a man has the last word in an argument, it's the start of another argument. John also claims the two best words in an argument are "Yes, Dear."
   —**Rick from RDW**

A Little Larceny in All of Us

BY BOB LEY

Let me count the ways...

A group of merchants at a local eatery at lunchtime were sharing war stories.

From a women's store manager. "I always show an increase in clothing 'taken on approval' right before a big dance or civic event. A lot of it comes back the next morning. *Sorry, I just didn't like the color.* All the tags are pulled off."

The diners nodded that they understood.

"I have a customer who always takes things he wants to buy out in twos. He'll keep the higher priced one and return the lesser one…but with the tags switched. We catch it most of the time but he gets it by some of the younger help at times."

From a menswear merchant. "I can always tell when the high school is doing yearbook pictures. It's fun to look at the yearbook later and see how many sweaters that *just didn't fit right* were good enough for a photo shoot!" he offered with a laugh.

A hardware dealer tells of having several gallons of white paint returned, only to find later they had been partially used and refilled with water.

Rev. Caine added, "I even see a little deception in

church. One of my parishioners has made an art form out of folding three ones in such a way it looks like a huge pile of them. Probably makes him feel better when the usher puts the basket in front of him."

Of course, we've read accounts of people walking out of dressing rooms wearing much more than they went in wearing. Then there are those folks caught wheeling a seventy-inch flat screen right out the front door…using the store's shopping cart!

Professionals often wear big coats, with extra pockets sewn inside.

As much as we enjoy hearing about these antics because they're about someone else (*We'd NEVER do anything like that!*) most of us have to admit there is a little, just a little, larceny in all of us.

The speed limit is posted at 25. Are we *always* under that?

The sign says you can't bring eats into the theater. Uh…does that include the can of Coke and two boxes of candy in our purse or jacket?

How many pens do we own that we didn't purchase?

Not exactly high crime that might land us in prison, but smiling at the gall of some takes on a little different color.

Check the following test to see how honest you are:

Do you…

Yes   No   Usually coast through stop signs when "the coast is clear?"

Yes   No   Automatically lay off the gas when approaching a police cruiser?

Yes No	Ever fudge your age?	
Yes No	Sometimes exaggerate your grandchildren's accomplishments?	
Yes No	Answer "This old dress? I've had it for years!" when complimented?	
Yes No	Ever fib a little about how little you paid for gas?	
Yes No	Take a few pound off *actual* weight when filling out a form?	
Yes No	Bought food at the deli to take to friends, but put it in your serving dish to disguise it?	
Yes No	Just cleaned what showed?	
Yes No	Told friends in Florida how nice it was here today (when it wasn't)?	

How many times did you say "Yes"? Here's your score:

7 to 10: *You seem pretty normal. Bet we'd be friends!*
4 to 6: *Maybe you didn't understand the questions.*
1 to 3: *Say a Good Word for me when you get there!*

And if anyone should ask…

Always remember, you're unique—just like everyone else.

FAVORITES

fa•vor•ites (fā′vər-ĭtz, fāv′**rĭtz**-) *n.* **1.** Things or persons thought of or treated with kindness or partiality, enjoying special favor or regard. **2.** Someone trusted, indulged, or preferred above others. **3.** Contestants or competitors regarded as most likely to win. *Syn: darlings, pets, idols, ideals, favored or adored or beloved ones, apples of one's eye.*

8LTRMAX

BY SAMUEL D. BESKET

Road trip, anyone?

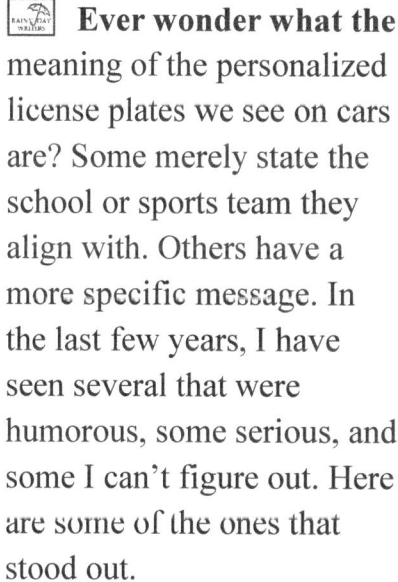 **Ever wonder what the** meaning of the personalized license plates we see on cars are? Some merely state the school or sports team they align with. Others have a more specific message. In the last few years, I have seen several that were humorous, some serious, and some I can't figure out. Here are some of the ones that stood out.

COOP-4-2… was on a BMW mini cooper car. My son-in-law has one. It's a nice car, but as the plate states, only 4-2.

MY-RET-MNT, KIDS-R-GON, SPENT-IT, KIDS-INHT were all on Corvettes. Then there was a fellow in a vintage corvette who had **LST-RIDE**. What a way to go.

SPOILED-1 and **NEW-DAD** were on small imports. I wonder how long it will be before New Dad will be trading for a minivan?

PA-8-MANG was on a SUV pulling into a parking garage at Heinz field in Pittsburgh. To add to the décor, four young girls, decked out in Denver Bronco gear, emerged from the car heading for the game.

HUSKER Gal on a Nebraska plate.

L8DBG…Lady be good and **HOW-U-BN** on cars driven by ladies. A lady driving a car with huge rust holes had **1-NOT-4-U.**

TRY GOD, CATHOLIC, METHODST and **FATHER** were on cars in Cleveland. Then one plate said it all: **HEZ-RISN.** Read this one fast.

HOG-PEN was on a truck painted to match Harley Davidson dealership colors; **LUV-BUG** on a Volkswagen beetle.

SNOW-ELF, ME-SAM, NURSE, and **GOT-RING** were on sporty cars driven by young girls.

KIL-TH-EX... I don't know how this one got by the BMV. Evidently, they had been through a bad break up.

2TOTHE8... Basically it means two to the eighth power. It has to do with bits and bytes in computer language. A bit is a number that has only two possible values. It's either a 1 or a 0 and can't be anything else. There are eight bits in a byte. The total number of possible values or states of a byte of information is therefore calculated to be 2 to the 8th power. That's 2 X 2 X 2 X 2 X 2 X 2 X 2 X 2, which is 256. I'm told the number 256 is all over the place in terms of what goes on at the innermost level of computers. I was lost after 2 to the 8th.

Bumper stickers

Driver carries no cash...he's married.
Honk if you love Jesus...text if you'd like to see Him.
Should vegetarians eat animal crackers?
Marriages performed by the Captain are valid for duration of trip.
Insanity runs in my family...in fact, it gallops.
My get up and go got up and went.
If you can read this...I lost the trailer!

If I Were a Flower

BY MARTHA F. JAMAIL

*But friendship is the breathing rose, with sweets in every fold.
(Oliver Wendell Holmes, Sr.)*

If I could be any flower, my choice would be a rose. Their palette of vibrant colors range from deepest scarlet to various shades of red, yellow, pink, and white…with a few hybrid colors thrown in the mix. Roses are sturdy and long-lasting from young bud to full maturity. They are not only lovely at every stage of bloom, but also filled with a delicate sweet fragrance.

Roses will grow as small plants in a flower bed, as full bushes, as small rose trees, and even as climbing vines. The roses in our flowerbed next to the house grow tall enough to peek through the picture window. We never cut them because they offer a permanent colorful bouquet throughout the growing season.

Roses are a popular subject for all of the arts. I'm one of many artists who have chosen roses as the subject of a painting. Roses have often been the choice for writers, poets, and musicians alike. They are also touted as the most popular gift for Valentine's Day, Mother's Day, birthdays, anniversaries, and hostess gifts. A gift of a single long-stemmed red rose is often valued as much as a bouquet of another type of flower.

Rose scents are the basis for many perfumes, air fresheners, and creams. They are chosen for colors and to name many types of cosmetics.

As if that weren't enough, roses can also be dried. My daughter-in-law's bridal bouquet of red and white roses is preserved in a lovely glass dome. When a rose has reached full maturity, its petals can be removed and pressed between tissues to dry. Then they can be used in still more ways—to create an entirely new frame-able work of art, or in a potpourri.

Yes, I think my choice to be a rose is a good one. Oh-oh! Ouch! Now if I could only do something about those prickly thorns!

A RESPONSE TO MARTHA
By Paeonia Lactiflora

In case you didn't know, Paeonia Lactiflora is the scientific name for me, the peony. Martha chose to be a rose! Really! Give me a break. Peonies have spectular blooms, and are much larger and showier than the common rose. Roses are so overrated.

Peonies also come in various shades of pink, red, and white, with hybrids of intense shades of coral, peach, and yellow. We, too, can grow as small plants, bushes, or trees, and our lovely leaves are vibrant and shiny. Our blooms are intensely full and large, sometimes compared to small cabbages!

Peonies don't need a lot of water, so we can pretty much take care of ourselves, unlike the needy rose. Our wonderful glossy leaves provide the nourishment for the next season's growth, and our leaf-covered buds provide tasty food for ants while they assist in the opening of each of our lovely blooms.

Why, just last year we were featured on the cover of Town and Country magazine with the headline, "Nothing makes a woman smile quite like a fresh bouquet of pink peonies."

The article also said that peonies should be in your

wedding bouquet because they are regarded as a symbol of good fortune and happy marriage. Another plus that may be unknown – we can live to be 100 years old.

So, Martha, do you still want to be a rose? Another plus is we don't have any thorns. Oh-oh! What is that tickle? Hmm…well, you might have to be on the alert for those pesky stray ants. Our tight blooms do make good hiding places.

A rose by another name

"An idealist is one who, on noticing that a rose smells better than a cabbage, concludes that It makes better soup." –H.L. Mencken, *A Book of Burlesques*

"If the English language made any sense, 'lackadaisical' would have something to do with a shortage of flowers." –Doug Larson

A man walks into a flower shop…"I'd like some flowers, please."
"Certainly, sir. What did you have in mind?"
He shrugs. "Well, I'm not sure. I uh, I uh…"
"Perhaps I could help. What exactly have you done?"

If you want to say it with flowers, remember that a single rose screams in your face, "I'm cheap!" –Delta Burke

Mom's BLT

BY SAMUEL D. BESKET

A meal to make your mouth water!

You may wonder why I selected a BLT sandwich as my favorite meal over a New York strip or grilled salmon. After all, it's nothing you can't order at any restaurant in town. The sandwich I'm talking about isn't your ordinary BLT, and one sandwich is a meal. It's best served in the summer when tomatoes and lettuce are available fresh out of the garden.

My BLT started with Mom dragging a huge slab of bacon out of the refrigerator. She would cut several thick slices and lay them in her hot, lard-greased cast iron skillet. I like my bacon crispy and enjoyed listening to it snap, crackle, and pop in the skillet. While this was taking place, I would select a large red beefsteak tomato fresh out of the garden. You need a slice from the middle of the tomato so it covers the whole slice of bread. Next came the lettuce, a head we had picked the night before that was chilling in the refrigerator. The real treat was if we had homemade bread, if not, white Wonder bread would suffice.

You start by lightly toasting the bread and spreading a thick layer of Miracle Whip on one side, then add about a half inch of lettuce. Next, salt the lettuce, then add a thick slice of tomato and a little more salt. The bacon was the last ingredient to add, about four slices. After one more coat of Miracle Whip, the sandwich is ready to eat. Now, firmly grasp the sandwich with both hands, cradling it in the palms to keep anything from falling out and, voila!—the perfect sandwich.

There was a pause in writing this story of about thirty minutes while I made a BLT. Alas, the lettuce came from a bag, the bacon was made from turkey, the Miracle Whip was made with olive oil, and the tomato was store-bought. Oh, how I yearn for the good old days!

Bacon bits

Bacon is duct tape for the kitchen.

I like my sarcasm like I like my bacon—laid on thick and aimed straight for the heart.

My Favorite Place

BY MARTHA F. JAMAIL

Oh, we ain't got a barrel of money
Maybe we're ragged and funny,
But we'll travel along
Singing a song,
Side by side.

An aroma of cigarette smoke wafts through the open doorway, and I know he is near. He doesn't smoke in the house anymore. We've been together now for more than 47 years—long enough that we often complete each other's sentences. Sometimes we even know what the other is thinking.

If you're lucky enough to be married to the same person from the fires of first love to the glowing embers of aging together, you are very fortunate. Those glowing embers make the best kind of fire. They burn slow and deep, inviting you close to their warmth.

From the first moment we met there was a special connection. He was in the Air Force on the other side of the continent, but he wrote to me every day. There was no social media at the time, but each letter was something tangible and personal that I could hold in my hands. I still have every one of them stored in a box of memories.

A beautiful sunset is an awesome sight, made even more so when I'm sharing it with him. We enjoy laughing at the same jokes, working together at home or at volunteer events, and, most of all, sharing the supreme joy of the birth of our two sons and now our grandchildren.

I know what you may be thinking—of course we had our disagreements. There were times when we both wished the other actually lived on the other side of the continent. But if you're willing to work through those moments, it's certainly worth it in the end. Life stokes the fire and keeps it burning.

Raising your children together is another strong bonding gift to parents. Our greatest joy now is seeing that same love flourish in our sons and their wives. Now with their own children, they understand the true meaning of love.

You may have guessed it by now but, if not, I will tell you. No matter where we are, or what we're doing, my favorite place is with my husband.

Starry-eyed love

"It wasn't love at first sight. It took a full five minutes." –Lucille Ball

"Love is a fire. But whether it is going to warm your hearth or burn down your house, you can never tell." –Joan Crawford

"I love being married. It's so great to find one special person you want to annoy for the rest of your life." –Rita Rudner

"People who throw kisses are hopelessly lazy." –Bob Hope

HEALTH

health (hĕlth) *n.* **1.** The overall condition of an organism at a given time. **2.** Soundness, esp. of body or mind; freedom from disease or abnormality. **3.** A condition of optimal well-being. **4.** A wish for someone's good health, often expressed as a toast. [ME *helthe* < OE *hāelth*.] *Syn:* vigor, haleness, wholeness, good condition, healthfulness, good health, fitness, robustness, bloom, soundness of body, freedom from disease or ailment, lustiness, stamina, energy, euphoria, full bloom, eupepsia, salubrity, constitution.

A Honey of a Cure

BY BEVERLY WENCEK KERR

Nobody's sweeter than my Granny...

At Granny's house, there were two general cures for everything—whiskey (used from toothaches to bullet wounds) for the men, or honey for everyone else.

Almost everyone has a jar of honey at home that they use to sweeten their tea or spread on a slice of buttered toast. That sweet taste is one we know well, but most people don't think about it as part of their medicine chest.

A bottle of honey seemed to hold magical powers for many aches and pains. But Granny only purchased honey from George, a local beekeeper. Not all honeys were created equal, so Granny wanted George's honey when she needed to use it to assist with medical problems. George could supply her with raw honey, which was full of antioxidants. His honey had never been heated or pasteurized.

Here are some of the old time uses for the all-natural ingredients of honey that Granny thought worked well. Sometimes, she combined it with another natural ingredient for even better results.

Sore Throat. When one of the grandchildren woke up with a sore throat, Granny gave them a spoonful of honey. This soothed the throat by coating it with the fructose of honey, which is a fantastic antibiotic.

Cough. If they didn't tell Granny about the sore throat in the morning, by evening they might start coughing. Then, a combination of honey and apple cider vinegar in equal portions would be given to the child every half hour until the cough subsided.

Hair Care. Sometimes when Granny was going someplace special, she wanted her hair to shine. So she mixed a teaspoon of honey with five cups of water (or two tablespoons of coconut oil), and used it much as you might use a conditioner today. When it was rinsed off, her hair took on a special glow.

Scratches. Let's suppose little Johnny got scratched when walking through the woods. Some disinfectants would sting or discolor the skin. Instead, Granny washed the scratch, then applied a coating of honey, a great antiseptic, much like Neosporin.

Minor Burns or Sunburn. If she saw you had a sunburn or a minor burn, she'd put a coating of honey on the area, as it moisturized the skin. Honey actually kills dangerous infections and accelerates healing. Add a little aloe vera for calming the pain of burned skin.

Facial Cleanser. Honey can even be used as a facial cleanser and help fight off skin problems. Granny recommended this to teenagers especially. Take a half teaspoon of honey, warm it between your hands and then rub it all over your face. Leave on for ten minutes, and wash off with warm water. Many teens have used this successfully to help heal their acne and thanked Granny for the tip.

Energy Boost. "Forget energy bars," she told everyone. Before your next workout, take a teaspoon of honey because it enhances athletic performance.

Fruit Salad. Let's not forget that honey magnifies the flavor of fruits. When Granny made a fruit salad she combined a couple of her favorite fruits, such as cantaloupe and nectarines, then tossed them in a couple teaspoons of honey. That's much better and healthier than artificial sweeteners.

Honey is a healing gift from nature. This isn't something new. Honey was the most popular ancient Egyptian healing remedy. Hippocrates, the father of modern medicine, used honey as a treatment for pain, dehydration, and fever.

Each person in the United States consumes an average of 1.5 pounds of honey each year. There are over 300 kinds of honey produced in the United States. An average bee colony will produce about 60 pounds of honey a year. Look for raw honey at your farmers market or health food store.

Just in case Granny gave the boys too much whiskey for their ailments, honey was also a good way to relieve their hangovers. A few tablespoons of honey, which is packed with fructose, helped speed up their body's metabolism of alcohol. Guess Granny used honey for everyone!

When you went to Granny with a problem and she said, "Honey," she wasn't just sweet talking you.

Arthritis treatment using potato juice

Raw potato juice is considered one of the most successful treatments for rheumatic and arthritic conditions. It has been used in folk medicine for centuries. The traditional method of preparing potato juice is to cut a medium-sized potato into thin slices, without peeling the skin, and place the slices overnight in a large glass filled with cold water. Drink the water in the morning on an empty stomach. Fresh juice can also be extracted from potatoes. A medium-sized potato should be diluted with a cup of water and drunk first thing in the morning.

The Real Skinny on Fat

BY MARTHA F. JAMAIL

Diet—the four-letter word we all despise.

Why are we so obsessed with it? It's only a little three-letter word, F-A-T, and yet it commands an industry making billions and billions of dollars. Every form of media touts methods, equipment, recipes, drinks, pills, and even condiments to get rid of fat.

Wait, I've just gotten started—there's also hypnosis, bariatric surgery, liposuction, cosmetic surgery, body creams, plastic suits, weight loss foods, and even packaged meals shipped right to your door! In addition to TV ads, commercials, and shows dedicated to weight loss, there are enough diet books to fill a library.

My special favorites are the colorful magazines strategically placed at checkout counters. Competing for your attention while you wait in line, their glossy covers shout headlines of quick and easy weight loss plans next to mouth-watering photos of rich desserts. The unsuspecting buyer will purchase the magazine for the weight loss program often buried skillfully behind articles with more photos of decadent desserts. The mixed message is very well planned you see because, seriously, the industry would suffer a great loss if you ended up not being fat, or not caring that you were fat.

Here's a sure-fire method to tell if you're really fat and need to lose weight:
1. Has your physician advised you to lose weight for your health?
2. Do you need a seat belt extender on an airplane flight?
3. If you sit in a patio armchair, when you get up, does the chair come with you?

Alright, one of these is a little tongue-in-cheek, but I know some people who have become so preoccupied with their weight that it actually consumes their lives and may even be detrimental to their health. My advice—forego the gimmicks. Eat real foods you enjoy, but in smaller portions. Avoid between meal snacks. Count your blessings instead of calories. Walk whenever possible—it's an easy and effective exercise. Set goals and accomplish all you can to make life better for yourself, and others. Remember, when you die your weight won't matter as much as how you made other people feel.

Remedies for canker sores

Eat more yogurt. Active cultures in yogurt encourage healing and minimize further occurrences.

Apply ice to sooth pain and reduce inflammation. Effectively stop canker sores by applying ice regularly as soon as you feel symptoms.

Swish a couple tablespoons of plum juice in your mouth for a few minutes.

HISTORICAL

his•tor•i•cal (hĭ-stôr'ĭ-kəl, stôr'-) *adj.* **1a.** Of or relating to the character of history. **b.** Based on or concerned with events in history. **c.** Used in the past: *historical costumes.* **2.** Important or famous in history. **3.** Diachronic. —**his•tor'i•cal•ly** *adv.* —**his•tor'i•cal•ness** *n. Syn:* past, old, ancient, antique, bygone.

Orphan on the Tracks!

BY RICK BOOTH

Derailed, but not the end of the line.

The world we live in today is almost unimaginably different from the world our ancestors lived in a hundred and more years ago. In doing historical research, I am often struck by the dangers and difficulties people endured and accepted as "normal" long ago. Once in a while, reading through old newspapers with Internet search tools, I come across a particularly touching story from that vanished world that can't be forgotten; that lingers in the mind; that asks more questions than it answers; that calls for further research. What follows is one of the most poignant short stories from an old Jeffersonian newspaper that I have ever read, followed by the research the Internet fortunately enabled me to do afterwards, completing the story with a surprise ending that did not disappoint.

From the Cambridge Jeffersonian newspaper, July 26, 1906:

> SAW SLEEPING LAD TOO LATE
> And Engineer was Unable to Avoid Striking Him. Reginald Corrothers Dangerously Injured.
>
> Reginald Carrothers, aged about fourteen years, was struck by west bound B&O passenger train No. 7, due here at 6:02 a.m., Thursday morning at Mineral Siding, receiving injuries which it is feared will result fatally.

Young Carrothers is employed at the Cambridge Glass Plant and worked there until 4 o'clock Thursday morning after which hour his movements are not known. It is supposed that he boarded a freight train, intending to go to Senecaville where he has an uncle, but had been put off the train at Mineral Siding and being fatigued went to sleep on the end of the railroad ties. He was not seen by the engineer until it was too late to avoid hitting him.

After the accident the train was stopped and the injured lad placed in one of the cars and brought to this city. Dr. Winnett, of Barnesville, was a passenger and did all he could to relieve the lad's sufferings. On the arrival of the train here Bair's ambulance was called and the boy was removed to the Pacific hotel on Dewey avenue, South Cambridge. Dr. C. A. Moore, the B. & O. railroad surgeon, was called and later Drs. Cain and Hixon.

His left thigh was badly crushed and the left leg fractured between the ankle and the knee. He was also injured internally. He was unconscious most of the time, but recovered sufficiently to tell his name and where he lived, but did not tell what he was doing at the place of the accident.

He was a son of Mr. and Mrs. Charles Corrothers, both dead, and lived part of the time with his grandfather, Hosea Sigman, at Stop No. 6 on the Cambridge-Byesville street car line.

This seems the sort of story which, if written as fiction, would bring reprimands to a screenplay author for being too contrived—too much tugging at the heart strings— too unbelievable to be real. But it all really happened in Cambridge in 1906! It's bad enough that a child gets hit by a train any day, but the poor boy was sleeping on the tracks. Why? Because he'd been removed from a freight train while trying to get home in the middle of the night, exhausted. And why was he traveling in the middle of the night? Because at age 14, he was working the graveyard shift at the Cambridge Glass Plant! And why was that? Probably to support himself, because he was an orphan trying to get by while living with relatives! Not only that, but the train badly mangled him. He was in agony, in and out of consciousness, and surrounded by strangers at a cheap trackside hotel in Cambridge where a doctor checked his injuries and expected only the worst. That was no way for a poor orphan boy to die! I personally found the scenario so amazingly depressing in the worst Dickensian sense that I just had to do the research to find out what happened next. Did he live or die? And if he lived, was it for long? Was he a cripple for life? Did this accident ruin his future, if he even had a future at all? This story was just too haunting to leave be. Fortunately, the Internet answered all!

Because the name "Reginald Carothers" is a very rare one, research into his later fate was made easier than if he'd been named, say, "John Smith." Excellent research websites like ancestry.com, newspaperarchive.com, and findagrave.com all returned instant hits on the name, and nearly the best possible results showed up. The poor orphan boy did not die! Here is his story:

Reginald Lee Carothers was born in Byesville on December 26, 1891, the son of a coal miner named Charles Carothers who had married Mattie Sigman, the daughter of Hosea Sigman, with whom Reginald was apparently living at the time of the accident. By 1900, though, his family had moved to Lancaster. It is not clear exactly when his mother died, but his father passed away in late September, 1905, and was buried in Columbus. That is probably when he was sent to live with relatives back in the Guernsey County area. It was only ten months after his father's death that he was working the night shift at the Cambridge Glass Plant.

Hopping on and off freight trains was a not uncommon way for some people to travel back then, although if caught by a conductor or brakeman, the result was usually ejection from the train. With no other good way to get home at four in the morning, Reginald likely hopped a freight train going in the direction of a relative's house, and then was discovered and put off at a stop a few miles east of Cambridge. Exhausted, he apparently fell asleep too close to the track.

The Pacific Hotel to which he was taken after the accident was on Dewey Avenue on the opposite side of Wills Creek from the Cambridge Depot, approximately where today's Speedy Print business is located. It would not have been a good place to die. Fortunately, he survived.

In later life, Reginald often went by the nickname Ray, as reflected in many of the online records that can be found about him. By 1910, he was living back in Lancaster with the family of a stonemason named Jones. There he was working for another glass factory, likely the Hocking Glass Company which was the ancestor of the Anchor Hocking Company.

What, though, about his awful injuries? Was he crippled? Apparently not. His 1917 WWI draft card stated he had all his limbs and no known disability. He was living in Columbus by that time, working for the Hocking Valley Railway. (Apparently he had come to terms with trains well enough to work with them, despite the accident.)

Reginald "Ray" Carothers ultimately lived to the age of 66, but his life was not without further sorrows. He buried three wives before the fourth one buried him. And no, none of it was suspicious. He married Lena Clark Axline, a widow with one child, in 1917. (Lena's first husband had died in a 1912 farm accident, run over by a harrow when his horse team panicked while planting rye.) She, unfortunately, died in 1923 from an ectopic pregnancy gone horribly wrong. She's buried in Pataskala.

Ray picked up the pieces of his life and married Anna Leonard. By 1931, they were living in Newark, and he was working as a Metropolitan Life Insurance agent. The company gave him a leadership award that year, too.

It appears from the records that he and Anna had moved back to Lancaster by 1934. In that year, he was serving as a Scoutmaster for Scout Troop 23 in nearby Haydenville. A newspaper reported that his troop would be demonstrating the game "Skin the Snake" at a Scout gathering in Columbus that spring. In Lancaster, he was once again employed in the glass business, presumably for the same company he had worked for in 1910. He registered for the WWII draft in April, 1942, and was described as a blue-eyed blonde who was 5 feet 8 inches tall and weighed 178 pounds. Two months later, unfortunately, Anna died, and he was left a widower for a second time.

Once again, he recovered and married a woman named Sylvia Cush, whom he may have met at work. She was an Anchor Hocking "assembler," and he was categorized as a "machine operator" there at the time. When the war was over, he made another career switch to become a real estate broker in the Lancaster area, operating under the business name "Ray's Realty." Sadly, on Christmas Day, 1952, his third wife, Sylvia, died.

Widowed three times, Ray soldiered on and found his fourth wife, Hazel Siwek of Akron, who joined him in Lancaster the next year. Just one year after that, in 1954,

Ray formally retired from the real estate business. The month he turned 65 in 1956, he made sure to apply for his Social Security benefits, too.

In 1957, Ray made his last move, this time to Newark near where his younger sister lived. Health and the need for family may have been partly motivating that relocation, since he died in the hospital at Newark the next year, on October 6th, 1958.

Reginald "Ray" Lee Carothers lived far longer than the doctors at the old Pacific Hotel in Cambridge ever expected. He came back from death's door to live an apparently healthy (even if unlucky with the wives) life, fit enough and caring enough about others to serve as a Scoutmaster for another generation of young boys. He gave back. His obituary stated that he had two grown sons, Leonard of Lancaster and Charles of Cincinnati, and two grandchildren.

And so it was that the orphan on the tracks, the most piteous character I've ever run across from the annals of old Cambridge, survived. He thrived through thick and thin, gave of himself, and lived a very full life, not without its sorrows, but most certainly also not without its triumphs. He died a husband, a father, and a grandfather. He was interred at Forest Rose Cemetery in Lancaster, the place where he had likewise buried his second and third wives. His last wife, Hazel, is not there, nor can I find records of her elsewhere. I suspect that she, like Reginald, moved on and remarried.

The informational bonanza available for family and historical research on the Internet today is almost breathtaking. I had only hoped to find that the poor orphan on the tracks did not die in a seedy trackside hotel, alone in the midst of strangers. Thanks to the Internet I found so much more — a life filled in with so many reassuring details, a full life, a life apparently lived quite well. I still don't know what became of his last wife, Hazel, though, but I'll not spend too much time worrying about that. I'm sure she moved on and did just fine. And besides, she was never an orphan on the tracks!

Robbing Brooklyn blind(s)

From *Frank Leslie's Illustrated Newspaper* of July 26, 1856, we learn of a fantastic little swindle. It seems that the residents at 73 Hicks Street, Brooklyn, rented the house from Mr. John Taylor. Around noon, a man drove up in an express wagon, told the residents that Mr. Taylor had sent him over to pick up the window blinds so that they could be repainted. Much pleased with the generosity of their landlord, the tenants helped load up the wagon with every set of blinds in the house. Neither the blinds nor the wagon driver were seen again.

The Duck Pond Disaster of 1896

BY RICK BOOTH

Bringing new meaning to the term 'madder than a wet hen.'"

Most people have heard of the famous Johnstown Flood which occurred when a dam broke in 1889, flooding Johnstown, Pennsylvania. It killed more than two thousand people. Yet nearly all memory has been lost of the "Miniature Johnstown Flood" which struck Cambridge, Ohio, on July 27, 1896. The Cambridge City Park Pond, commonly known as the Duck Pond, was the culprit. Assaulted by an intense night of wind, thunder, and rain, the waters of the already swollen pond overtopped the dam at its southern end and quickly eroded a six-foot-deep gorge through it. Several acres of pent-up water rushed down through the lower sections of the north side of town. The damage done was considerable.

The Jeffersonian newspaper reported, "The water came down with such force that practically everything in its way was carried off. Small houses, fences, board walks and chicken coops were swept away." The "small houses" swept away were likely sheds and outbuildings as no human casualties were reported, but it's a good bet that a number of citizens wondered the next morning where their privies had gone.

The pond's dam had been built a few years earlier on the estate of Colonel Joseph D. Taylor, the area's politically influential retired U.S. Congressman, who was also probably the richest man in Cambridge. Among his earlier construction projects were a large Wheeling Avenue office building at Seventh Street; the Berwick Hotel at Sixth, which he actually built twice since its first incarnation was destroyed by fire; and his beautiful Victorian mansion on the hill just west of the pond. All these structures still survive, as does even the repaired pond dam, which now lies beneath Sherman Avenue between Eighth and Ninth Streets. But what greeted his eyes the day after the storm was an empty lake and a twelve-foot-wide gap in the earth that was originally meant to retain it. He quickly had workers repairing the breach.

The storm of 1896 wrought even more damage on Cambridge than just the dam break. The convenience of heating and lighting with natural gas had come to town about a decade earlier, so when lightning struck a gas regulator housing just east of the city, it caught fire, spewing flames that were seen for "quite a distance."

The people who perhaps came nearest to severe injury that night were Mr. and Mrs. Jed Williams. He was a local marble and gravestone monument merchant. Lightning struck and destroyed the chimney of his house, showering bricks into the bedroom where Jed and his wife were sleeping. Luckily, though some bricks fell at the bottom of the bed, neither of them was hurt.

Lightning also struck a horse stable on the south side of town, but at least it didn't burn the place down. Furthermore, the bridge over Wills Creek at the west end of Steubenville Avenue was imperiled by the high water as one of its abutments threatened to fail.

All in all, the record storm of 1896 was one the residents no doubt remembered and talked about for years, not unlike the way everyone who was in Cambridge in 2012 recalls the devastating windstorm that came through that year too. Yet with time, memory of the 1896 event faded. All the damage was repaired. The tragic Johnstown Flood occurred seven years before the dam break in Cambridge, but it is remembered and memorialized to this day mainly because of the tremendous loss of human life it involved. Our local "Miniature Johnstown Flood" was not of the same magnitude as the one in Pennsylvania. It torched a gas installation, shattered a chimney, shocked some horses, threatened a bridge's structural integrity, and washed out the Duck Pond's dam. Yet no one was injured or killed. The event was ultimately forgotten, but not because there were no deaths involved. Indeed, there were a few, but the casualties all were chickens!

Carry on, my good man.

Member of British Parliament: "Mr. Churchill, must you fall asleep while I'm speaking?"
Winston Churchill: "No, it's purely voluntary."

FEATURE ARTICLE

On Being a Grandfather

BY BOB LEY

It all looks different from the top.

Visions of adventure and bravery in the skies over Europe were what I best remember of my grandfather. Born in Scotland and raised in England, he would tell me wondrous stories of life in the Royal Air Force, a fledgling outfit in 1916. He was recruited to pilot training in the middle of the First World War.

Wood framed airplanes, covered with painted muslin, with huge, oil belching engines made up the RAF. Two passengers, the pilot in front, the gunner behind him, used their wits and skill and daring to fly over the German trenches, flying low enough that the gunner had a chance to hit his enemy with his handheld 'Tommy' gun.

The roar and speed of the planes must have been a frightening sight to the enemy, most of whom had not even seen an airplane. The planes flew so low that the Germans would throw two by fours into the air, hoping to be high enough and timed to hit a propeller or tear away the skin of the plane.

His stories included machine guns built into the plane, timed by gears to fire between the propeller blades, doubling the available firepower. Occasionally a gear would jump, causing the gun to shoot off the propeller.

Pilots and gunners, if hit by enemy gunfire, were usually shot in the legs or backside. My grandfather fitted the two seat bottoms of his plane with a heavy lead shield… then promptly flew into some trees when the plane would not climb quickly with the added weight. No damage to the pilot, except to pride.

Running low of oil midway through the war, the Brits used castor oil in the crankcases, causing severe bowel problems to the passengers from breathing the fumes in the open cockpits. All the dashing pilots depicted by Hollywood did not compare with the real scene… pilots running to the outhouses located along the runway as soon as they touched down and could manage to halt the plane.

There were so many stories. I found them fascinating, seeing this side of what I considered then to be an old man, and begged him to put them into writing, or to at least record them. He always said he would, but he passed away at age ninety nine not having done so.

When one of my grandsons asked me what life was like "in the old days" the temptation was to ignore the question. I couldn't possibly live up to my grandfather's spectacular life. I still have a silver cup he received for having won a motorcycle race in 1920!

I thought to myself, *"How could I ever live up to that. However, you are doing just what your grandfather did."*

One evening I decided I would give it a try. I sat down and typed the following letter, intended for him and those who might be interested.

Dear Kids,
One of you has asked what my life was like "in the old days," spending most of my life in Cambridge, Ohio. Far different than yours, I am sure.

There were no interstate highways, very few four lane roads in fact. Travel was difficult even for those lucky enough to have a car. I am not talking wagon trains here, but not everyone owned a car, even though a new Ford could be bought for less than six hundred dollars. When I got my driver's license, gas was eighteen cents a gallon, but coming up with a dollar was another challenge. A trip to Columbus was an event! We planned for days where we would eat, what stores (besides Lazarus) we wanted to see.

There were no Visa or Mastercards then, so we had to be sure we had enough money for the trip, and whatever emergencies that might arise.

Saturday nights were big events in downtown Cambridge. This was the shopping center for the entire county and the farm folks spent the day doing their business at the Court House and shopping for the week, perhaps eating at one of our many restaurants. The streets were packed. Aggies was a favorite, but there was the Coney Island, Stone's Grill, the Central Restaurant, the American Restaurant, the Guernsey Dairy Bar, a little later came the Kopper Kettle, and several others. Fast food restaurants, McDonalds, Wendy's and the like had yet to be invented.

I am sure your generation wonders how we got along without FM radios, tape decks, CD's, iPhones and all that. We listened to our favorite programs on the radio and there were a bunch of them: The Lone Ranger, the Green Hornet, Inner Sanctum, Ozzie and Harriet, Amos and Andy. They seemed so real at the time.

Then there were the Saturday matinees. Most often they were Western movies, with a newsreel shown first and often a "Perils of Pauline" short feature, with Pauline left tied to the railroad tracks and the locomotive bearing down, followed by 'to be continued.' Of course that encouraged going again next Saturday!

We played sports, usually pickup games in the

neighborhood. We had a Little League and a Biddy League football program, and we were issued a coveted shirt with the sponsor's name on it. Your cousin just recently signed up for seven-year-old soccer. He had to buy a complete outfit for $85.

Traveling teams didn't exist. We played against the local kids.

Converse was the tennis shoe every kid hoped to have. Casey's, Alexander's (home of the merry-go-round), Gallenkamp, Keystone Shoes, Turnbaugh's were all shoe stores available downtown. There was no Walmart or K-Mart. Shoes had to last too, and Cambridge was blessed with Tom Justice and Carey Burris, two expert shoe repair men.

Kids, I am glad we can still talk together because the language has changed so much and I am not doing well at keeping up. I thought of 'grass' as something to be mowed, 'coke' was a cold drink, 'pot' was something my Mom cooked in. It amazes me you guys can still write a sentence after I read some of the texts I get. 'LOL', 'C U', 'Luvya', and so on.

Donohue's Bike Shop was in the basement of what is now the People's Bank. A great place for dreaming, especially for the Bridgestone motorbikes they sold. They looked like motorcycles but didn't require a driver's license. A guy can dream a little!

Another block down, about where the US Bank is now, was Vance's Bait Store...an interesting place to visit if fishing was your thing.

Kresge's, Newberry's, and Woolworth's were all five-and-dimes located in our downtown. Amazingly, many items were actually five cents and ten cents. Two had lunch counters, all three carried a variety of goods and were valued because shopping was made easier for us by having them handy. Kresge's even had a large fish tank and sold goldfish.

Talk about a complete shopping experience!

When your grandmother needed new clothes, Cambridge offered lots of selection. At the top of the scale was the Style Center. Also available was Morton's Millinery, Jean Frocks, Casual Shop, B. Goodman's, Rose's Department Store and j.b. clothestree.

Bonham's Department Store (known earlier as Davis Department Store) was the anchor store in the downtown, carrying upscale clothing for men and women, bedding, towels, china, and so on. Montgomery Ward was another large store that offered a wide variety of goods and, of course, there was the iconic J.C. Penney store.

We could do it all right downtown, a short walk for most of us.

I am aware, kids, that it must seem odd or quaint to you that many people seldom got out of Guernsey County. Why on earth would anyone choose to stay here, you think? After spending most of my life here, I suppose I am qualified to answer.

Before the advent of the interstate highway system and the proliferation of the automobile, Cambridge was the center of most things in the county. Our shops and stores offered a wide variety at most any price range. My thought is, why would anyone want to leave?

To experience Christmas in downtown Cambridge in the fifties, with snow flurries in the air, the stores and streets decorated for the season, the music of the season played in every store and business, the joy on the faces of the shoppers, was an experience I am sorry you missed. The restaurants and stores were packed, yet no one grumbled about the service. Most of the clerks were friends and neighbors and took an interest in helping you. Not as a salesperson, but as a friend.

To me it doesn't seem that long ago, but I well remember being your age and thinking seventy was ancient! I guess we didn't have a lot of what is considered indispensable these days.

There was no such thing as air-conditioning, television, ball point pens, or clothes dryers.

J.C. Penney and Sears Roebuck and Co. each had a gigantic catalogue put out twice a year. Their arrival was looked forward to by most every woman in the county. They were a place of dreams, a place to get anything not available in Cambridge. Orders would be sent by what you call "snail-mail", as computers had not yet been invented, and they would arrive by mail or freight, depending on the size of the order.

By the way, sending a letter took a three cent stamp. Postcards were called penny postcards for the obvious reason.

One of our neighbors was the first around us to get a television. The screen was almost round and, of course, was black and white. The antenna had to be moved for each channel. (Cambridge got three channels if the weather conditions were favorable.) He was kind enough to invite all the neighborhood males to his house to watch Rocky Marciano fight Jersey Joe Walcott.

My dad was a few minutes late and Rocky had knocked out Walcott in less than two minutes! There was no such thing as 'instant replay'!

As I left their house, I said, "Thanks for inviting us over, Bill. I really enjoyed it." Dad cornered me immediately.

"He is Mr. Bibbee to you, Robert, as is every man older than you!" It reminds me of how much has been lost in manners. Just recently a young man no older than twenty at Quicklube said to me, "Getcha in about five minutes, Bud." I decided not to correct him! (My name isn't Bud.)

There were standards like this that were expected of us and to be honest, it gave a certain order to life.

It afforded every person a dignity. I guess it was our form of political correctness, in place long before the current meaning of the words. It was before gay rights, computer dating, daycare, and time sharing. It wasn't all bad. Being taught to understand if we were doing something wrong meant we should expect consequences.

We were taught to respect police officers and men in the military. Serving was an honor and there was no greater place to live than Cambridge, Ohio, in the United States of America. They made it possible.

When I went on a date, it was a special thing. Shoes were shined, pants and shirt were pressed, a bath and my hair washed, and then I wore the best clothes I had. Girls did likewise. Most of the time we went to a movie, and then to Aggies for a Coke afterward. Often it was my father who did the driving. Things have changed a bit.

Politics was not the big money game it is today. Of course there was no television giving 24/7 coverage of every hiccup. Most of the advertising went to newspapers and radio. A popular method of getting in touch with the people was whistle stops. The candidate would board a train and crisscross the country stopping almost anywhere a small crowd would gather. The candidate and his entourage would stand on the rear platform and give a brief speech and take off again.

I was privileged to see three presidents that way: Eisenhower, Johnson, and Nixon.

Young ladies who found themselves in a "family way" were often sent away to relatives during their pregnancy. It was a matter of shame for many parents. Often, a missing father was "in the service" or some other excuse. That has certainly changed and to be honest, I am not sure which is better. Just last week, I saw a female television host who was not married being the recipient of a baby shower on her program.

Divorce, too, was nowhere near as rampant as today. Almost every family had a mother and a father. That meant there was much less welfare too. School breakfasts and free lunches didn't exist. I suspect they weren't needed as much as they are now.

Another thing I had that seems to have disappeared is front porches. During the summer months, we sat on the porch and talked to neighbors walking by, often couples with a baby carriage and a little tyke or two. We knew all our neighbors, helped each other in any way we could, but did not seem to intrude on anyone's life. People new to the neighborhood often, on move-in day, got a home-cooked meal from one, a warm apple pie from another as a welcome.

I guess it wasn't too exciting, but that's the way it was "in the old days" and quite honestly I don't think I would trade it for any other way.

Love, Grandad

As I read this over and think about it, it leaves me a little disappointed that my grandchildren will not see the joys that I had. But they will see their life as different as I see mine and hopefully will relish the good times. No doubt there are plenty of benefits to living in the computer age.

There is more information on the internet than one could possibly absorb in a lifetime, right at our fingertips! Things are done faster and often better with computers. Most of our large businesses could not exist without them.

Not long ago, I ordered a cabinet from one of the big box stores. It came in damaged. I went to the business to tell them and she dove for her computer.

"We have another one in Bexley. Do you want to run up there and pick it up or have one sent here next week?"

A two hundred mile round trip and she (a lot younger than me, but who isn't?) acted as if it was across the street.

Why don't we have cities like Cambridge used to be? We often hear the complaint there are no "real" stores here anymore. It's called "progress." The ease of getting a hundred miles and back in one afternoon makes a business accessible to thousands more people, promoting the so-called big box stores who do a regional business, not needing a store in every city in the nation.

Customers can find even larger selections than they could in the fifties in a small town, forsaking the smaller stores that once filled our Main Streets.

Is it better? My grandfather felt his generation had it together. I felt mine did. I am sure my grandkids will be no different.

It's a generational thing

My granddaughter came to spend a few weeks with me, and I decided to teach her to sew. After I had gone through a lengthy explanation of how to thread the machine, she stepped back, put her hands on her hips, and said in disbelief, "You mean you can do all that, but you can't play my Game Boy?"

MENTORING

men•tor•ing (měn′tôr-ĭng) *v.* **1a.** Making easy or easier. **b.** Giving wise counsel. **c.** Teaching. *Syn:* instructing, guiding, coaching, teaching, training.

Mentoring

BY DONNA J. LAKE SHAFER

Definition: Mentor: (mĕn'tôr', -tər) n. experienced and trusted advisor.

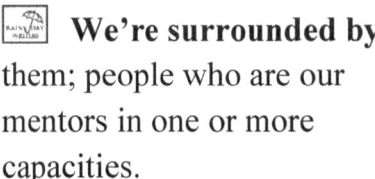 **We're surrounded by** them; people who are our mentors in one or more capacities.

Your parents were your first mentors. They were mentoring you since you were a small child, often repeating the same list of "do's and don'ts" until you got it. What to eat, when to eat; when to bathe; when to go to bed, when to get up; how to dress, how not to dress; how to address your elders. How to choose a mate, how not to choose a mate. How to make money, how to spend money and how not to spend your money and so on. Their advice is probably still ring in your ears today. They were giving you the benefit of their ages and vast experiences.

Advice, advice, advice. Some of it solicited, some not. Some by well-meaning folks, but not always. You'll have many mentors just by chance and circumstances. Your school teachers, for example, and many other adults during your childhood and adolescence. But when selecting a mentor for your needs, you must seek out those experienced in his or her field of expertise. You'll have many during your lifetime. Ministers, bankers, medical professionals, attorneys, to name a few.

Other folks may show up in a mentoring capacity when least expected. Maybe a relative, an old friend, or even a stranger who offers helpful suggestions for a perplexing problem; a solution entertained before it was pointed out to you. We need to take this information, knock it around for a while to see if it, or any of it, fits. Weigh the pros and cons and the most likely outcome. Then make a decision or seek a different point of view from still another mentor.

We all need to pick the brains of others at times. Don't be afraid to ask. It's not a sign of weakness but one of strength. After all, although some may try to give the opposite impression, no one knows everything, but chances are there is someone who can give your questions a wise and thoughtful answer. You may need guidance in matters of career, health, education, finance, mental health, religion, philosophy, love and marriage…seek one who can guide you to the greatest success in whatever you attempt to accomplish.

Your mentor, whatever the need, will be someone you admire and respect.

So, "listen up and listen well."

Listen up

"Sainthood emerges when you can listen to someone's tale of woe and not respond with a description of your own." –Andrew Mason, physician

All-American Work Ethic

BY BEVERLY WENCEK KERR

Raising them up right.

Children have inborn qualities that guide them throughout life. Sometimes parents and teachers try to guide pupils to what they think would be best for them. But often the youngster already knows.

At the age of seven, Bruce cut his parents' yard. Always attracted to things that he could ride, three-wheelers and four-wheelers played a big part in his life. His travels took him all over Old Washington.

In the evenings, Bruce and his dad would work on his dad's truck or lawnmowers. They worked well together. His dad taught him to always do what he could, if anyone needed help.

When a neighbor down the road in Old Washington needed someone to mow her lawn, Bruce gladly volunteered. Even though he was only twelve, he could ride down the side of the road a few houses away. Soon a neighbor of hers asked Bruce to mow her lawn also. His business was already beginning.

Being too young to drive, but with a driving force to make money, his parents provided transportation and a little assistance for his new project. Word spread about not only the nice appearance of the lawns he trimmed, but also his honesty and willingness to work. Summer after summer, his business continued to grow.

This young man saved his money so he could purchase his own mower, truck, and trailer once he finished his education. He never even advertised his business. It grew by word of mouth.

During high school, this industrious young man participated in OWA, a work/study program where students actually had a paid job for a portion of the day. That way, he would earn money to save for his business. It's no surprise that favorite classes included Vo-Ag and Industrial Arts.

Upon graduation from Buckeye Trail, Bruce already had a large base of satisfied customers, who appreciated the care and detail put forth to make their yard the best looking yard in the neighborhood. He took great pains to be sure that everything was trimmed, sidewalks were blown free of grass, and flowers were not disturbed.

Cindy, his sweetheart since high school, worked alongside him on a daily basis. They had a beach wedding at the Outer Banks on the family's annual vacation there. Neither of them ever stops working and they are instilling that great work ethic in their two children, Andy and Lillian.

This lawn care service continues today, twenty years later, but it has expanded from 34 yards when he was fifteen to 230 yards today. Bruce said, "They're more than just customers. They seem like a family connection."

Once in a while they have an unusual experience.

For instance, a cemetery that they mow may be haunted. Several times when they have mowed there, a belt has jumped off the mower. The same song often repeats itself on Cindy's iPod. They've even seen a figure moving slowly through the tombstones.

Bruce and Cindy work extremely hard for about seven months out of the year doing lawn care. Usually, he repairs his own mowers and trucks unless there just isn't enough time. In the winter, he even does some carpenter work.

Ever since Bruce was a child, his dad taught him to help everyone. One evening coming home, they got delayed between yards for some unexplained reason. As they were coming up the hill, they met a man mowing along his fence line and the mower rolled into the fence just as they passed. Of course, Bruce and Cindy stopped and hooked up a chain to right the tractor. They were there at just the right time.

Now he gives employment to other young men who want to make some extra money. But the work is hard and during the summer they may work from six in the morning until eight in the evening. His reason for success can best be expressed in Bruce's words: "By the blood, sweat, and tears of all of us."

There's not much time for anything else except Andy, Lillian, and the farm animals. Andy plays baseball and basketball and has time for 4-H and Cub Scouts. Lillian takes gymnastics and dance lessons. They're one busy family.

Winter gives him time to enjoy his family and their farm, where they raise several kinds of horses, goats, and even a couple steers so they can have their own beef. While he may not be rich, he earns more than most of his previous classmates and, most importantly, finds happiness in his work.

This example of an old-fashioned all-American family refreshes the spirit. The four of them do everything together, from working on the farm to mowing and playing. At the end of the day their hands might have calluses, shoulders could ache a little, and the joints feel stiff, but they wouldn't trade their life for anything.

Each person must find his passion so he will be free to enjoy life. When you are doing a service for others, you are rewarded in many ways.

Author's Note: This young man happened to be my student many years ago. It's always a pleasure to see what students do with their lives. And, yes, he does cut my yard and even secured my totem pole to the shed.

--Bev

Hoodathunkit?

Money is the side effect of work.

A Lesson from Mr. Tom

BY SAMUEL D. BESKET

It was a place where a kid could learn more than just the nuts and bolts of the hardware business.

Mr. Tom owned the local hardware store in my town. Every small town in Guernsey County had such a store in the fifties. This was a time before superstores or the home improvement stores we have today. I've been told that such stores did a thriving business when coal mines dotted the countryside decades ago. By this stage of his life, it was a hobby for him. He ran the store to have something to do.

One day he asked me if I would like to work a few hours a week in the evenings or on weekends. This began a process I still remember.

He started me off by having me clean up, sweeping the floor of his store and warehouse. Gradually, he elevated me to where I could wait on customers. Mr. Tom stressed honesty, integrity, and making sure people received good service.

A lot of his hardware was delivered in bulk: nails, sand, gravel, and pipe. When I arrived, he would give me a list of pipe to cut to length, nails to weigh out, and sand or gravel to shovel into his truck.

One day a customer arrived with his own truck and ordered five hundred pounds of sand. As I started to walk across the street to his warehouse, Mr. Tom cautioned me to watch him. "If he sits in the truck when you tare out the truck weight, make sure he sits in it when you load it." Sure enough, the fellow sat in the truck as I tared it out, and then got out as I started to load it. When I thought we had around five hundred pounds, I asked him to get back in the truck so the weight would be correct. He did this and, as I finished loading the truck, Mr. Tom showed up just to see how things were going. Somehow I believe he was somewhere watching all the time. Later that day, he said. "Not everyone is honest; sometimes we have to help them a little."

An embarrassing moment came when I overcharged a customer two cents for a pound of nails. I figured the tax wrong. Mr. Tom had me go to the man's house to return the two cents and to apologize. I never forgot that lesson and always double-checked my addition after that.

Helpful hardware man

Question: A man is doing some work on his home and goes to a hardware store. He goes up to the clerk and tells him what he wants. The clerk tells him that each one is $1. He tells the clerk he would like 5000 and he is charged only $4. What did he buy?

Answer on page 213.

The Day I Became an Artist

BY MARTHA F. JAMAIL

A nun gives a nod.

That day is forged in my memory. It was September, 1956, at St. Elizabeth Parochial School in Clarksdale, Mississippi. Located in the heart of the delta region, the intense heat of summer continues well into the fall season.

Our classroom was oppressively hot that day, in spite of the rhythmic thumping of the ceiling fan. Every student was deep in thought, solving 7th grade math problems. If we finished the assignment, our only alternative was to quietly read a book. Doodling, drawing, or otherwise using your pencil during free time was frowned upon. Reading was paramount, and using the pencil sharpener during class time was considered a noisy distraction.

Our teacher, Sister Ruth Virginia, was a nun in the Order of Sisters of Charity. No student ever complained about the heat because of Sister. She was always dressed in a long-sleeved, floor-length black habit with an attached elbow-length cape. Her head was covered with a starched white cap, which framed her face.

My assignment was completed, and my book was boring. Across the aisle from me, Chuck diligently continued to work on math problems. He was so intent on his assignment, I thought he would make a perfect model.

Quietly, I slid a sheet of blue-lined notebook paper from my folder and began to draw his profile. In order to keep my pencil sharp, I alternately used the side of the lead point and blended in shadows with my finger. I smiled at how quickly Chuck's likeness was beginning to appear on my paper.

Suddenly, I became aware of Sister standing at the front of our aisle. She quickly approached my desk and stopped. Too embarrassed to look up, I moved my hands away from the drawing, revealing my sinful transgression. After an agonizing moment of silence, Sister walked to the back of the room. Stealing a furtive glance, I saw her remove a key from her pocket which she used to open a cupboard. I quickly faced front again, wondering what punishment I'd receive.

Sister returned and, without saying a word, placed a large sheet of creamy manila drawing paper on my desk, then continued to the front of the class. In that very special moment, she validated me as an artist.

An artist's eye

"Every child is an artist. The problem is how to remain an artist once we grow up." –Pablo Picasso

Back Then

BY JOY L. WILBERT ERSKINE

What a difference a few decades makes!

Back then, even as a little five-year-old girl, walking to kindergarten by yourself was just something you did. The first time, Mom walked the route with me—down the road, around the corner, past the big bottling plant, several blocks farther, and then through the playground to the school. From that day on, it was my job. I felt like a big girl, entrusted to do something all by myself. Mom and Dad never had to think twice about sending me out the front door alone. No one ever bothered me along the way. Imagine that!

All of us kids were pretty independent. Oh, that's not to say we weren't shy sometimes—after all, we knew our place and were taught manners…but we weren't scared to try new things or be off on our own for hours. It just felt natural to be a kid, using our own imaginations to have fun with friends and learn new stuff. We figured we could do just about anything we wanted.

That sometimes got us into a pickle, like the time we were looking for something on Dad's workbench in the shed. I don't remember what it was, but there were three of us there, earnestly searching high and low for a tool for some project or another, when my brother suddenly popped up with it in his hand. Trouble was, I was leaning over him at the time—his head connected hard with my jaw, my jaw snapped shut, and my tongue just happened to be in the way of my teeth. Split my tongue sideways clear across the middle and...well, you get the picture. That meant a trip to the emergency room, me spitting and crying all the way.

Those kinds of things happened, but they were just a part of living. I healed. Never thought to blame my brother or mother. Didn't develop a lifelong fear of workbenches. And never even considered suing anybody.

The occasional alligator or boogieman under the bed was more of an issue than the real world, and even that was more about the thrill of feeling scared. We knew there were no monsters under the bed, but we checked anyway, just to be sure. I remember jumping from my bed to my sister's so I could peek underneath mine without having to touch the floor or dangle my head in harm's way. We usually solved our own problems like that. Mom and Dad were always there when we needed them, but we were expected to look for our own solutions too. It was good growing up. We developed a sense of responsibility, feelings of self-worth, and pride in a job well done. We learned to tackle our monsters and subdue them.

We roamed the neighborhood wherever we wanted. People didn't care if you cut across their yard or played cars in the sand in their driveway. Property lines only showed up on legal papers. But if you caused any trouble, you answered "Yes, Ma'am" or "Yes, Sir," to whatever adult reprimanded you (and they did). And your parents backed them up 110 percent. We learned at a young age that we would pay the consequences for our actions.

Long after dark, we played outside. The only rule was you had to stay within shouting distance. When Mom called, you came running home. And she only called once (maybe twice in case you were playing too hard to hear the first time). I can still hear our young voices in the twilight: "I gotta go home now. Mom's calling me. See you tomorrow." Disappointed, maybe, but not disobedient. Obedience was rewarded with trust and trust resulted in expanded freedoms—you figured that out pretty quick.

Life was pretty simple back then. We loved, learned, trusted, obeyed, and grew. Our parents loved us enough to let us learn for, and master, ourselves. My, how times have changed.

What a pickle!

My three-year-old stuck out her hand and said, "Look at the fly I killed, Mommy." She was eating a juicy pickle at the time, so I thrust her contaminated hands under the faucet and washed them with antibacterial soap.

After sitting her down to finish her pickle, I asked, with a note of awe, "How did you kill that fly all by yourself?"

Between bites, she answered, "I whopped it with my pickle."

Prodding from a Friend

BY HARRIETTE MCBRIDE ORR

True meaning of a "good scout."

In the 1940s, while attending Ninth Street Elementary in Cambridge, we were invited to join the Girl Scouts and become Brownies. My best friends all were joining and some of their mothers were to be our leaders. One fireball behind the organization was Alice Eikenberry, the mother of my dear friend Mimi. She had six children and taught school at Garfield Elementary. She volunteered for many organizations.

I grew to love being a Brownie and then a Girl Scout. I was a Scout during all of my school years. Mrs. Eikenberry was always there.

Attending a banquet one evening, she came to me and said, "You need to volunteer as a Girl Scout leader at "Camp Hill 'n Dale."

"My children are not old enough to be Scouts."

"Well, we have babysitters for your children. They will be well taken care of and we really need you. You have gone through the whole program and you know the ropes."

Needless to say, she wouldn't take no for an answer.

In a short time, there we were one morning, myself and three little ones, headed out Route 209 to "Camp Hill 'n Dale." I left camp early each day to be at work at Champion Spark Plug by three p.m.

That was the beginning. Alice prodded me along and, the first thing I knew, I was a leader at Lincoln Elementary and then Washington. We had the largest troop in Cambridge.

I took training at Camp Tilting Acres in Zanesville, in order to qualify to take my girls on overnights.

On meeting days, I dragged myself out of bed and forced myself to wake up to be ready in plenty of time for an after-school time of fun. We hiked, cooked over an open fire, learned the Girl Scout laws, and always had a craft project at each meeting. There was never a dull moment.

My assistant leader called one morning, saying her neighbors had moved during the night. "Did you get our cookie money?" she asked.

Needless to say, our cookie chairwoman and our money had disappeared into the night, never to be seen again.

When "Camp Fire" came to Cambridge, my children were in college. Alice again called me. I became a leader and later a member of the Camp Fire Board. As president of Camp Fire, we sold pizza at the Salt Fork Festival and our council, for the first time, ended the year in the black.

Many of the friends I made in Scouting became lifetime friends. They were also involved in the Salt Fork Festival. One thing led to another, and soon I was spending a week of my vacation volunteering for the festival.

Mrs. Alice Eikenberry prodded me on to an interesting life of volunteerism, the same kind of life she aspired to. Thank you, Alice.

The Old Piano Roll Blues

BY BEVERLY WENCEK KERR

Tickled to tickle the ivories.

Perhaps you recall the joy of watching an old-fashioned player piano, where old familiar tunes came forth as if by magic. As a six-year-old, Michelle always enjoyed visiting Freda, who lived a couple miles from their farm. Freda had such a piano.

While Michelle's parents visited with Freda and Charlie, Michelle sat fascinated as roll after roll entertained her on that old piano. The keys magically moved as the songs played. Sometimes Michelle would sit on the piano bench while pumping the piano pedals, and pretend that she was playing the songs while moving her hands over the keys.

One day when they went to visit, Michelle could hear the sounds of music from the driveway. When they went to the door, she could see inside and Freda was actually playing the piano herself. She was playing a loud song and hitting the keys harder than seemed necessary.

Once they rapped on the door, Freda looked around, seemingly embarrassed. "Oh, I didn't hear anyone coming up the drive. Come on in."

"Is everything alright?" Mom asked, as Freda seemed very upset.

"Not exactly, but it'll be okay. Charlie's tractor broke down this morning and I'm not sure how we're going to have the money to fix it. He really needs it to plow the fields. For some reason, when I get upset, I take it out on the piano and play a loud tune."

Michelle thought about this for a while, then went to the kitchen where her Mom and Freda were having coffee. "Freda, do you ever play soft music?"

"Why, yes, when I'm happy I like to play a soft and happy tune. Music soothes me one way or another. It's better than medicine to help relieve problems."

At home, Michelle pretended to play the piano on the kitchen table. When happy, she moved her fingers lightly with the songs, but when upset, she would hit the table using great force with her small fingers.

One day when Michelle came home from 4-H, a big surprise waited in the living room. A brand new piano from Hellstern Music Store seemed to beckon her to tickle the ivories. No longer would she be playing at the kitchen table.

Years later, she talked to Mr. Hellstern about her piano. He told the story of how her dad came to his store wanting a piano for his table-playing daughter. Mr. Hellstern told him, "If she wants to play that much, she needs a piano." So he kindly made arrangements with her dad to pay $5 a week from his small pay at Cambridge Glass Company.

Michelle still remembers the excitement of her new piano even now, although she's a grandmother today. Running her fingers over the keys, even if they are slightly out of tune, still comforts her and makes her very thankful that long ago someone gave her a special gift that developed her love for music.

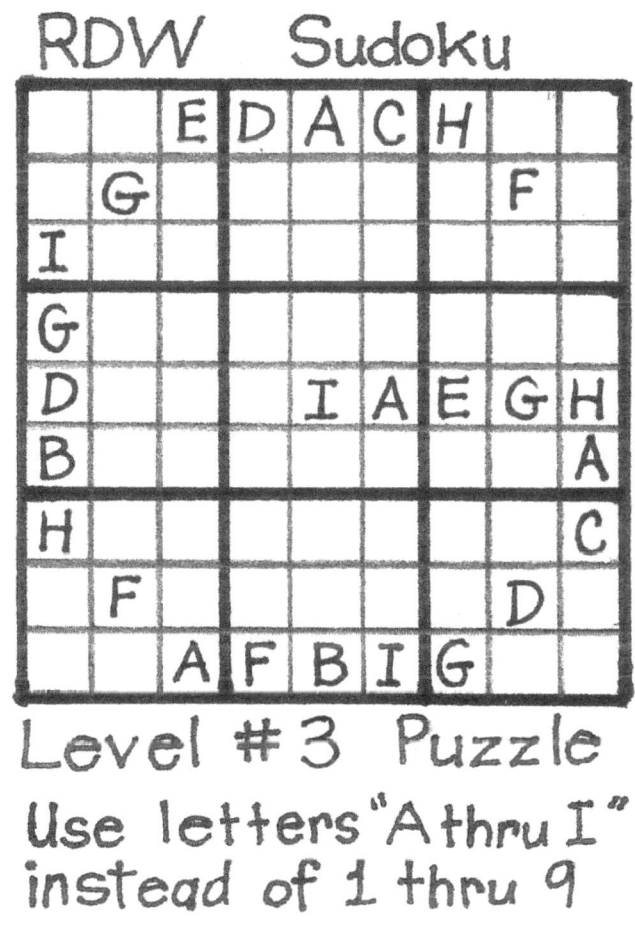

Solution on page 213.

Sister Veronica

BY BOB LEY

What did a woman, let alone a nun, know about cars?

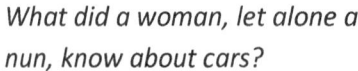 **She was five-ten.** I learned at an early age that estimating a female's weight, even if she was a nun, earned few style points. Let me say it was substantial.

This was Sister Veronica, a Dominican nun, and my eighth grade teacher. Just the sight of her cruising the hall of the Catholic school, black and white garb billowing around her as she walked, was an imposing sight.

She was quick to assess my lack of interest in scholarly pursuits. In retrospect, I would guess most any teacher would pick up on that rather quickly. As a young teenager in the fifties, my all-abiding interest was cars. Even though I could not legally drive, I had purchased an old Chevy, with hopes it would be ready by Emancipation Day…my sixteenth birthday! Most of the time spent on the Chevy was in lieu of doing homework.

One day in late September, Sister Veronica asked me to stay after school and talk to her. "You're not in any trouble, but we need to have a conversation before you are!" she proclaimed, which is how I came to be sitting at a desk facing her. We worked out a deal. "I expect you to get all, and I mean *all* A's and B's, nothing less," she intoned, "and I will help you work on your car."

I tried not to laugh. Her intentions were good. What did a woman, let alone a *nun*, know about cars?

However, I worked on my end of the bargain and Sister Veronica began presenting me with various articles she had clipped from who-knows-where about mechanics, body work, racing, show cars, cars of the future, and so on. I feel sure she surreptitiously tore pages from *Mechanics Illustrated* and *Hot Rod* at the public library. On four consecutive Saturdays, she gave up her days and installed new upholstery in the Chevy. Of course, I worked harder than ever in my life not to let her down.

Her approach to education was certainly unique. On many evenings during that winter, it being too cold to work on Betsy (her name for my car), I would stop at the convent. Inevitably, she would round up a couple more nuns and challenge me to Scrabble. Of course, the words I used had better be well thought out.

No one dared to tease me about her. Not that *I* was feared, *she* was!

In May, Sister Veronica announced she was being recalled to Wisconsin. It was devastating but, looking back on my year, it was more than just her mentoring. I regarded what she did in the classroom as teaching. What she did outside the classroom, and I discovered later I wasn't the only one she worked with, was truly mentoring.

She also taught me that by caring, greater things are possible. By giving of yourself, you get others to give back. That is mentoring.

It ain't on the parts list

The other day I was in the local auto parts store. A lady came in and asked for a seven ten cap. We all looked at each other and one of the service guys asked, "What's a seven ten cap?"

She replied, "You know, it's right on the engine. Mine got lost somehow and I need a new one."

"What kind of car do you drive?" another guy asked. (Thinking that perhaps she drove an old Datsun Seven Ten.)

The lady replied, "I drive a Buick." We asked her how big the cap was. She made a circle with her hands, about 3-1/2 inches in diameter.

"What does it do?" asked one of the service guys. She replied, "I don't know, but it's always been there."

One of the guys gave her a note pad and asked her to draw a picture of it. So she drew a 3-1/2 inch circle and wrote 710 in the center. As she was drawing, the guys behind the counter looked at it upside down and fell behind the counter, laughing their heads off.

(Get it? Draw a circle and write 710 in the center. Now look at it upside down.)

The Person I Would Like to Meet

BY MARTHA F. JAMAIL

Fame is fleeting, but anonymity can last a lifetime. (Joe Johnston)

In today's world, meeting someone can be as easy as touching the screen on your cell phone or typing a few letters on your computer keypad. Instantly, you will receive all kinds of information about the person you want to know. Unfortunately for me, the person I would most like to meet is the anonymous author of the poem, "The Teacher."

The Teacher

Lord, who am I to teach the way
To little children day by day
So prone myself to go astray?
I teach them knowledge, but I know
How faint they flicker and how low
The candles of my knowledge glow.

I teach them power to will and do
But only now to learn anew,
My own great weakness thru and thru.

I teach them love for all mankind

*And all God's creatures, but I find
My love comes lagging far behind.*

*Lord, if their guide I still must be,
Oh, let the little children see,
The teacher leaning hard on Thee.*

This poem was and still is an inspiration for me. I came across it back in 1970 while completing an assignment for a Children's Literature class at Muskingum College. The teacher told us to collect 100 poems as part of our course requirement. I believe that poem was the only one labeled "anonymous" in my collection, and actually was my favorite. I referred to it each time I was required to give my philosophy of teaching.

I wanted to meet the author to find out more about him or her…if the author were a teacher or had been inspired by a teacher; what the author's life was like; and what he or she enjoyed doing. I wanted to know if the author was a writer or had just penned this poem.

Anyway…last week, during a phone call with my sister, I shared with her what I had written and my dilemma. She asked me to give her the title and first line of the poem. Within seconds, she found the author's name and background on Google.

Leslie Pinckney Hill was an African-American, born in 1880, the son of a former slave. He was an educator, author, poet, dramatist, and community leader. His poem "The Teacher" had been translated into several languages. Mr. Hill believed that education could be used to fight racism. I, too, believe that education is one of our cherished freedoms, empowering us to become productive citizens not only for ourselves, but others as well.

After finally getting to "meet" the anonymous author online, I wondered who the "smarties" were who did all the research for Google. I actually asked that question of Google and it responded that they had an extensive research staff, and that most of them have PhDs in their fields of expertise. The site also provided an application form! Thanks anyway, Google, but I am just a lowly non-techie with a bachelor's degree. ☺

And a special thanks to my sister.

Helpful hint

On the last day of the year, my first graders gave me beautiful handwritten letters. As I read them aloud, my emotions got the better of me and I started to choke up.

"I'm sorry," I said. "I'm having a hard time reading."

One of my students said, "Just sound it out."

MILITARY

mil•i•tar•y (mĭl′ĭ-tĕr-ē) *adj.* **1.** Of, relating to, or characteristic of members of the armed forces. **2.** Performed or supportedby the armed forces: *military service*. **3.** Of or relating to war: *military operations*. **4.** Of or relating to land forces. *n.*, pl. military also –ies 1. Armed forces. 2. Members, especially officers, of an armed force. [ME < Lat. *mīlitāris* <*mīles, mīlit-,* soldier.] **--mil′i•tar′•i•ly** *adv. Syn:* armed, martial, militant, fighting, combatant, soldierly, combative, concerning the armed forces, noncivil, warlike, for war.

Knittin' for Britain

BY DONNA J. LAKE SHAFER

To knit or not to knit? A young girl's answer to a knotty question.

It was the late 1930s when the girls in my fourth grade class, along with those in the fifth and sixth grades, were advised that we would be taught a new skill. We would learn to knit. Knit? Knit? I, for one, had no desire in learning to knit. Mother didn't knit, neither did Grandmother knit; so what was the point? I had done a little embroidering and soon learned that I didn't care for it and had no reason to think knitting would be different. My interests leaned more toward reading, bike riding, roller skating, sleigh riding, tree climbing, and attending Saturday matinees at one of the local theaters.

Soon it was explained to us that a war was raging in Europe and our adult friends and many children in England were often cold. We would knit 8- or 10-inch squares, I forget which, and then some nice ladies, maybe Red Cross volunteers, would join the pieces together to create an afghan, whatever that was. Except for newsreels, we had no concept of the war, but we understood cold, as some winters in southeastern Ohio could be rather bitter.

Soon, we were supplied with yarn and needles and

received instructions in the art of knitting. No purling, just knitting. Cast on, go back and forth, over and over again until the piece was the right size, and then cast off. In time, we were gaining experience and, except for a few dropped stitches which were corrected with the help of a crochet hook, we got rather good.

In time, we began to take pride in what we were doing, making those little squares that, when united, would provide warmth for some otherwise cold folks. We felt that we were helping in a war effort that was becoming more and more familiar as the days wore on. There's no telling how many school children in this country engaged in this practice. But it's safe to say that there were many. I don't remember if there was a program for the school boys to engage in at that time but, as for the girls, there was a lot of "knittin' for Britain."

Years later, I took up knitting again. Like riding a bicycle, you never forget how, but now it was for a guy serving with the United States Air Force in another faraway land. This time, instead of squares, it was black socks, complete with his white initials knit into the toes. I learned to purl, turn a heel, cable stitch, and later could even create argyle socks. A few years later, there were warm and sometimes colorfully patterned sweaters for my kids, both boys and girls.

That reminds me. I started a sweater for myself about ten years ago, then lost interest. Maybe I'll flush the thing out of storage and finish it.

Or maybe not. I'll have to think on that a bit.

Life in the Military

BY SAMUEL D. BESKET

I can't hear you!

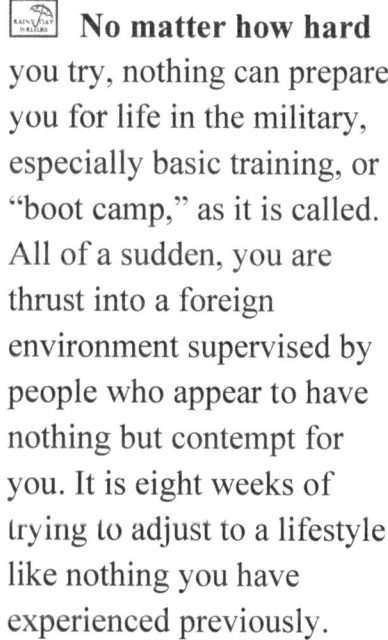

No matter how hard you try, nothing can prepare you for life in the military, especially basic training, or "boot camp," as it is called. All of a sudden, you are thrust into a foreign environment supervised by people who appear to have nothing but contempt for you. It is eight weeks of trying to adjust to a lifestyle like nothing you have experienced previously.

Upon arrival at the "welcome center," as it was called, we were greeted by one hundred and sixty pounds of spit-and-polish training instructor. Ironically, his name was Sgt. Pope. Believe me, he was the total opposite of any papal figures I have ever seen.

The first thing he did when he saw us was slam his clipboard to the ground. Then he went on a rant like none I had ever witnessed. He paced back and forth in front of us, cursing and screaming. Then he got right in our faces and screamed obscenities and racial slurs. He didn't care what color you were or your nationality; no one was exempt from his remarks.

He referred to us as a bunch of $&#&@% rainbows, in reference to our clothes being different colors. "Don't unpack your bags," he said. "Half of you won't make the cut."

One of the first things we learned was to run. If we weren't marching, we were running. Even if the distance was very short, we ran.

The second thing I learned was no one talked in a normal tone. All the communication we received from the T.I. was loud and vulgar.

After a few weeks, we began to gel; our alignment and marching was better and we began to feel like a team. This was all accomplished through repetition. If one trooper got it wrong, everyone did it over again. It didn't take us long to shape up the slackers.

At the end of our first block of training, we had our first inspection in Class A uniforms. In the Air Force that means dress blues. The previous night was spent ironing our uniforms, squaring away our foot lockers, and spit shining our boots. I don't know where it came from, but a bottle of Johnson's Liquid Wax miraculously appeared. A few drops on a cotton ball did wonders for our boots.

We knew they would find something wrong during the inspection. The thing to do was try to minimize it. But it didn't matter, even a small infraction was treated drastically. If a footlocker didn't pass inspection, it was turned upside down. If they couldn't bounce a quarter off a bed, it was stripped. With every infraction, you were issued a demerit, or *gig*, as we called it. Once you accumulated more than the allotted amount, you were set back a week in training. That meant moving to a new squadron, something none of us wanted to do.

Once a week, we had commander's call. That was when our squadron commander, or 'the old man' as we called him, talked to us about our training. One of the first things he did was have us write a letter home.

After a few minutes of critiquing our training, he surprised us all by saying we could go home if we didn't like the Air Force. "Just raise your hand," he said, and we could go home, no strings attached. I was really surprised when a few fellows held up their hands. I had a dozen uncles who served during World War II. There was no way I could go home.

The next morning after formation, the fellows who held up their hands were asked to fall out. I don't know where they went; we never saw them again. Sgt. Pope told us they went home to their mommies. He also told us that didn't fulfill their military obligation, indicating their names would be returned to their local draft boards. So much for no strings attached.

After eight weeks, we graduated from phase one of training. Those of us selected to attend tech schools received orders to other bases. The others remained to finish their training, then on to OJT (on-the-job training).

Our last day in camp was busy. We had our last formation, packed our duffle bags, and reported to the orderly room for final instructions. One by one, we were called in for a final word from Sgt. Pope. When I entered the room, I saluted, stated my name, and stood at parade rest. When he told me to sit down I was shocked, almost afraid to, but he insisted. His attitude and demeanor were more pleasant. It was the first time I heard him talk in a normal tone of voice. After a critique of my records, I was dismissed to leave through a side door, waiting for the rest of the squadron.

When the interviews were complete, we marched in loose formation to the departure center, located next to the welcome center, where our trials had begun eight weeks earlier. Sgt. Pope shook hands with all of us, wished us "God speed," and disappeared into the welcome center. Shortly, a Greyhound bus arrived and disgorged another bunch of recruits. We kind of chuckled among ourselves, knowing what was in store for them.

A few minutes later, to our surprise, Sgt. Pope emerged from the building. Walking up to the group of new recruits, he paused and slammed his clipboard to the ground. He then went into his prearranged rant, screaming and cursing everyone, just like he did us eight weeks earlier. Fortunately, the bus then pulled up for us to board. We were more than happy to go.

Sign me up!

Airman Jones was assigned to the induction center, where he advised new recruits about government benefits. It wasn't long before Captain Smith noticed Airman Jones had almost a 100% record for insurance sales, which had never happened before.

Rather than ask, the Captain stood in back of the room and listened to the airman's sales pitch. Jones explained the basics of GI insurance to the new recruits, then said, "If you have GI insurance and go into battle and are killed, the government has to pay $200,000 to your beneficiaries. If you don't have GI insurance, and you go into battle and get killed, the government only has to pay a maximum of $6000."

"Now," he concluded, "which bunch do you think they are going to send into battle first?"

One Military Family's Big French Adventure

BY JOY L. WILBERT ERSKINE

Charles DeGaulle did us a big favor.

Life as an Air Force brat was pretty darn good most of the time, but there were some occasions one can only appreciate in retrospect. Living through them…not so much.

It was near the end of my seventh grade year, in 1965, when Dad got an assignment for a three-year tour in Toul Rosieres Air Base. We were moving to France! Ooh-la-la! From that moment until early June, when we left Stead Air Force Base in Nevada, it seemed like we got another immunization every day. It was necessary because those shots protected us from whatever diseases we might catch in a foreign country, but toward the last I was feeling like a giant pin cushion. At last, the shots were done, Dad's sponsor had rented a house for us close to the new base, our household goods were packed and shipped, and we were on our way across the U.S. in the family van.

From Reno, it was a long cross-country trip to McGuire Air Force Base in New Jersey, where our flight would take off for Europe. Dad took a month's leave so we could stop along the way to say goodbye to relatives we wouldn't see for three years. Our car would be shipped by sea from a port near there and delivered about six weeks after we arrived in France. Dad always complained, "The worst part of the military is the 'hurry-up-and-waiting.'"

He was right. We did a lot of waiting on that trip. The morning of our flight, the seven of us were up and moving early. First on the agenda was getting the car turned in for shipment. That took forever, but by mid-morning it was done, and then we waited impatiently for the noon bus to the airport. We were all ravenous by the time McGuire came into view. Dad marched his little squad of travelers into the Snack Bar for a meal and then the wait began in earnest. I remember watching television for hours until our 9:30 p.m. departure time finally rolled around.

The flight to Frankfurt, Germany, would take seven and a half hours. We were assigned seats in the middle of the plane, right in front of the wings, where the view might have been fascinating if it hadn't been an overnight flight. We'd never flown over the ocean before and it would have been nice to see it. After a meal, we settled in for the night. In the seat behind me, I noticed a really cute boy and, typical teen, I daydreamed about what I might say to get to meet him, but it had been a long day and I fell asleep. By the time I woke up, we were almost in Frankfurt. We'd flown over London while we slumbered, so we missed that view too! I sure would've liked to see the city that spawned the Beatles, if only from the air. We could, however, look out the window and see the

German rivers sparkling in the sun. It was so beautiful! We discovered later that we'd been fortunate to land on such a clear day. Sunny days in Germany were rationed!

But we had arrived in Europe and life was good! The Frankfurt airport was huge! Busses took us from the runway to Customs, where we turned in our declaration papers and retrieved our luggage. We were briefed about being abroad and told not to expect the people to be like those we were used to. Now we were in *their* country and *we* were the foreigners. Surprised me, because I sure didn't feel foreign. Next step—waiting for the bus to take us to the train station.

We waited nearly all day. During this time, I became friends with a girl who had come over on the same plane we did. She and her family were going to Toul Rosieres too. It was nice to have a friend already in this strange new country.

Late in the afternoon, the bus finally motored in to take us to the train depot, where we arrived with barely enough time to jump on our train as it was pulling out of the station. The two suitcases I was carrying were hard to manhandle down the narrow aisle as we looked for a compartment to settle in. A German man literally screamed at us for being in his way. "Willkommen in Deutschland," indeed! I'd taken enough German to know what he said, and that wasn't it.

Germany's countryside is very pretty if you can get out of the rain long enough to get a good look at it. We had settled into two compartments, so we had a nice dry place to soak it all in over the 4½ hour train ride. At last, we crossed into France and began the last leg of a very long trip—the bus to Toul Rosieres Air Force Base.

By the time we arrived, it was getting pretty dark and we were tired, so we got rooms in the Bachelor Officers Quarters. The next day, one of Dad's new coworkers drove us out to our new home in a little town called Minorville, about six miles from the base, and dropped us off. The seven of us stood in a row on the "Grand'rue," and couldn't believe our eyes. Everything was filthy. A man dressed in dirty clothing, drove a herd of cows the muddy street that was the only road in Minorville. We would come to expect the cows every morning, noon, and evening. The smell was, simply put, nauseating…but we were American military and, like anything else that's difficult in military life, we knew we would get used to it. It's what you do.

The "house" in which we were to live was tiny—part of a rowhouse-type arrangement with a cow barn to the right and a dirty garage on the left. We were allotted two small bedrooms, a kitchen, and a bathroom (the bathroom, only because a GI who'd lived there before had put in a toilet). All five of us kids would be sleeping in the "big" bedroom.

In the back yard were pig sties and chicken coops. When big, mean mamma pigs nosed up to the one window in the back bedroom, we all jumped away. Below, in the cellar, we discovered more cow manure and carcasses of dead animals. The landlord later used this as a root cellar. Over our heads was a grain mill and the grain fell down into our house through cracks in the ceiling. We learned to ignore the rats up there in the middle of the night. Cow lice and beetles would be a new experience too.

The next day, someone from the base picked Dad up for work, and Mom and us kids began to clean our new quarters. We scrubbed all day. It was one tired family who sat down to a simple meal that evening when Dad got home. We were all ready to "hit the rack" when bedtime finally arrived, but the fun wasn't over yet. After midnight, Mom realized something was very wrong and roused everyone. She and Dad herded us out into the street—every one of us except Dad had terrible headaches and pounding in the back of our heads.

He and Mom decided we should go to the dispensary to get checked. We had no transportation, so Dad went to another GI's house in the village to get the man to drive us out to the base hospital. When we got to the dispensary, the medics immediately put us all on oxygen. We'd all gotten carbon monoxide poisoning, later attributed to a faulty wall water heater. I'd washed the dishes standing right in front of it and had gotten an extra dose. The medics said if we'd stayed in the house until morning we'd have all died.

The next day someone from the base came out to test the water heater before we could go back into the house. We never used the water heater again, just boiled water on the stove for everything. The water also tested foul. So until we left France, Dad carried drinking water from the base every day.

And that was our introduction to France! Over the next few months, there were some bright spots in our French adventures—we made good friends with neighbors, learned interesting things, did a little traveling around, and made some fun memories too. But seven months later, much to our joy and surprise, French President Charles DeGaulle kicked the Americans and Canadians out of the country—and we were ready to go!

French Customs

An elderly gentleman of 83 arrived in Paris by plane. At French Customs, he was struggling to find his passport. The Customs officer, a surly young man, said sarcastically, "You have been to France before, Monsieur? You should know enough to have your passport ready."

The American replied, "The last time I was here I didn't have to show it."

"Impossible. Everyone must show a passport on arrival in France!"

"When I came ashore at Omaha Beach on June 6, 1944, to help liberate your country, I couldn't find one solitary Frenchman to show it to."

You could have heard a pin drop.

The Lucky Ones

BY SAMUEL D. BESKET

To coin a phrase, he had a way with words.

Lessons I learned in basic training stayed with me for life. Directly across from our barracks were accommodations for people permanently assigned to our base. One thing that stood out was a patio, located in the middle of the facility. It had benches and picnic tables and several pop machines where residents could take a break and enjoy a cool drink.

Every day, we held our last formation across from this patio. For troopers who just came off a five-mile hike, the pop machines looked inviting.

"For every bottle of pop you drink, you lose a day of training." This was our training instructor's favorite saying and he harped on it every day. We thought he held these formations across from the patio to torture us.

One evening, as we lined up for our last formation, he surprised us. "Drop your packs. You have a ten-minute patio break." It was like a jail break. We fed quarters into the machines as fast as it would take them, and drank them just as fast. A few of the boys didn't have change. They were the lucky ones.

The ten minutes flew by and we formed up to march to our barracks, only this time he marched us to the drill field and started us to run. It didn't take long for troopers to fall out sick and vomiting. I was fortunate; I was nauseated, but everything stayed down. Finally, we formed up again.

"For every bottle of pop you drink, you lose a day of training," were his only words. Point well taken.

Listen up

The military has a long, proud tradition of pranking recruits. Here are a few tried and true winners:

Instructing a private in a mess hall to look for left-handed spatulas.

Sending a recruit to the medical supplies office to bring back a fallopian tube.

Having a young private conduct a "boom test" on a howitzer by yelling, "Boom!" down the tube in order to "calibrate" it.

Ordering a private to bring back a 5-gallon can of dehydrated water (just an empty water can).

MISCELLANEOUS

mis•cel•la•ne•ous (mĭs′ə-lā′nē-əs) *adj.* **1.** Made up of a variety of parts or ingredients. **2.** Having a variety of characteristics, abilities, or appearances. **3.** Concerned with diverse subjects or aspects. [Lat. *miscellāneus* < *miscellus*, mixed < *miscēre*, to mix. -- **mis′cel•la′ne•ous•ly** *adv.* **mis′cel•la′ne•ous•ness** *n.* *Syn:* heterogeneous, mixed, varied, assorted.

A Good Samaritan Surprise

BY MARTHA F. JAMAIL

A nudge in the right direction.

The early morning rain was icy cold on the drive to school and, unfortunately, was slowly turning to sleet…too late for school to cancel that morning. By the time I arrived, the teachers' parking lot had become quite slippery.

The sleet continued to fall, and by mid-morning the playground was as icy as a skate rink. We all wished the sun would come out and start the melting process, but no such luck. In fact, when the sleet changed over to light snow, the decision was made for early dismissal at 1:00 p.m. for all the area schools.

After the students were safely boarded on buses or picked up by parents, we teachers headed home. I dreaded the drive because our house is located on a hill with a very steep driveway. Actually, all went well until I reached the driveway. After three futile attempts, I decided to ask our neighbor if I could park in their driveway across the street. It was flat and wide enough that I would not block their access. As I got out of the car, Mrs. Thomas was standing at her doorway, smiling and waving.

She called out, "Honey, I was watching you try to get up your hill, and was hoping you'd just come over. You can leave your car parked here as long as you want."

"Thanks so much," I called back and, after a brief chat, headed across the street to a short hillside near a trio of mailboxes. I was hoping to be able to grab onto a mailbox for the final ascent. Unfortunately, the grass was iced over and, after only two steps up the slope, I fell backward onto the pavement. I immediately turned as red as my coat and looked around to see if anyone was watching. My second attempt was to try to run up the slope, but that ended just as badly.

For my next attempt, I tried to hold onto the mailbox and pull myself up, but it only got me halfway up, when suddenly I felt a push from behind and I was able to make it to the top very easily. I turned around quickly and, looking down, saw our neighbor's dog, Lassie, using her haunches to boost me up the hill. I could hardly believe it. That wonderful dog, so aptly named because she was a collie, had come to my aid. I bent down and gave her my best hug, and called to her to come to my door for a treat. She stayed just long enough for her snack and a final hug of thanks, then trotted back over to her house. I stood watching in grateful amazement until she disappeared around the corner.

Agatha's Mad

BY JOY L. WILBERT ERSKINE

A word to the wise...husband.

 Agatha would've forgiven Howard in a heartbeat, if he'd cared enough to ask. But he didn't. He just moved merrily on, happy to have his way, no matter what method he used to get it. She didn't mind doing what he wanted. It was just that he didn't ask her input before issuing an ultimatum. As long as he got what he wanted, it didn't matter if she liked it or not. That was the bottom line.

It was a minor infraction. He hadn't really made Agatha that mad, but she wanted to teach him a lesson. She didn't want to 'just get over it,' like so many times before. Men seemed to think it was pretty funny when they did something they knew their 'women' wouldn't like. *Oh, she'll get over it.* She'd overheard him and his friends say that to one another over a beer and a fishing pole out at Salt Fork. "Not this time," she muttered.

"Agatha, are you there?" Howard was puttering in the basement, not doing much, as usual. She moved across the kitchen to the head of the stairs to look down. He was standing at the bottom, staring up at her with a frustrated look on his face.

"Did Jack return my pipe wrench?" he asked. "I can't find it."

"He brought it right back. You remember, the Monday after Gus Macker. You were gone to Mr. G's, I think. You carried them downstairs when you got home. He returned the bits too."

"Can't find them either. In fact, I can't find several things. Have you seen the duct tape?"

"Did you leave it outside?" she suggested with a little smile. "Some days you're as forgetful as an amnesia patient on knockout drugs, y'know it?"

"Ah, I'll find them later," he grumbled, clumping up the stairs. He parked in his recliner, rattling the newspaper like he was wrapping fish. Agatha started washing dishes.

Fifteen minutes later, he was hollering again. "Agatha!"

"What, Howard? You don't need to yell. I'm only in the next room, y'know."

"Where's the remote?" he responded sullenly. "I can't find it and the news is coming on."

"It's probably right where you left it. Look around, you'll find it. You're the only one who uses it. It's got to be there somewhere."

Suppressing a satisfied grin, she heard him fumble through drawers and under cushions. In a few minutes, he flipped the TV on manually. She slipped the remote out of her pocket and stashed it in the closet with the tools he'd missed earlier. Overnight, she would replace those things and remove others that he'd miss tomorrow.

"This is fun." She muffled a giggle. "And if it makes him mad when he finds out, well, this time *he* can just get over it."

Think Pink

BY DONNA J. LAKE SHAFER

NASCAR ain't for sissies.

The green flag flashed and Michelle crushed the pedal to the metal. It was her first NASCAR race and she was the only woman driver. Jeff Gordon passed her on the left and Kyle Busch roared by her on the right. She'd raced against these two in other races, but that was a long time ago. Now Michelle was ready, for them and the forty other drivers in the race. A breast cancer survivor, she was up for the challenge. Decked out in a pink jumpsuit, a pink helmet, and driving a shocking pink Ford, she was ready for the second biggest race of her life.

Engines roared as gears shifted into second, third, fourth. Chevys, Dodges, and Toyotas were all finely tuned and ready for the big day.

As they neared the first turn of the simulated road course, Michelle set up her apex and downshifted, passing two cars. Coming out of the curve, she gained on Jeff and Kyle and passed three other cars as they headed down the straightaway. Later, the yellow caution flag was up and it was slow down time for everyone. Staying in position, they passed a blue Dodge that had spun out. Taking this time to catch her breath and plan her next move, Michelle gained the determination that had helped her through those terrible months of chemo.

Once again, the green flag was in motion, just in time for an upcoming U-turn. Downshifting and changing position, Michelle made it through the turn smoothly, gaining speed as she came out, once again heading for a long straightaway. Several laps later, she was closing in on her two closest competitors. Pulling up near them, she laid on the horn. Impulsively, both cars moved aside as she roared between them, leaving them several lengths behind as she sped away.

Surprise, surprise! shouted Michele to herself. *So you two clowns thought I was just a powder puff racer, eh? Gotcha! Read the slogan on the sides of my car, boys. THINK PINK. That'll teach you to underestimate this girl. You want to see me again? Check out the winner's circle. Toodles!*

And with that Michelle pulled away, leaving the two drivers in total embarrassment and wondering what the heck had happened.

Dressing for success

Donna and Harriette were having lunch at Mr. Lee's when Donna spotted a man wearing a blue and white striped shirt and a bright green sweater vest. That seemed like a strange combination.

A few minutes later, Harriette noticed another man coming in the door. This fellow was wearing a bright blue sweater vest. She commented, "Those kind of vests aren't worn often today."

Donna, who is never at a loss for words, shrugged her shoulders. "Maybe they're going to an investment meeting."

Fear...A Delayed Reaction

BY MARTHA JAMAIL

Everybody's an art critic.

 It was a perfect day for an art project on the enclosed patio. With two screen doors opposite each other and all windows open, the cool breeze invited itself in.

Earlier, my husband had brought in a large box with patio furniture from Big Lots. With more errands to run, he said he'd assemble it later. After he left, I noticed a bottom corner of the box was split open. The print next to it read "Made in Thailand." My first thought was I hoped no small pieces were missing.

After spreading an old tablecloth over my workspace, I began to mix pâpier-maché. It was quite a messy process, but soon it took on the quality of soft clay. My armatures were already made, so I began to apply the first layers. I was making a fish and a turtle for the local 3-D art show.

Time flies when you're having fun and, before I knew it, two hours had passed. The fish, formed on a wire hanger, hung off the left side of the table to dry, while I continued working on the turtle.

I turned at the sound of bicycles pulling into the carport. It was Susie and Teenie, two artist friends who had come to inspect my progress.

"You better have something to show us for your efforts—we're getting tired of riding around waiting for you!" Susie exclaimed.

"Where's the fish? I thought you were making a fish?" asked Teenie.

"It's here," I said, pointing to my left.

Susie walked over to look and screamed, "Sn-a-a-ke!!!"

It's still difficult to imagine how the three of us managed to get through the doorway together, but we did. Peering back through the screen, I could see the snake still coiled in the corner right next to my worktable. It must have come from the Big Lots box and been with me the whole time I had been working. If I had stretched my legs out, I would have touched it. We couldn't believe it still had not moved.

Our neighbor, Roger, hearing all the commotion, came over to inspect. He just walked around to the opposite screen door and propped it open. Our little friend soon slithered out. It was a bright coral color and about three feet long.

I couldn't wait to tell my husband the box of patio furniture actually did have something missing—a stowaway from Big Lots!

It's all in the perception

I discovered I scream the same way whether I'm about to be devoured by a great white shark or if a piece of seaweed touches my foot.

Wishing on a Star

BY BEVERLY WENCEK KERR

*Star light, Star bright,
First star I see tonight.
Wish I may, wish I might,
Have the wish I wish tonight...*

"Please let me take a boat ride," finished the small lad as he climbed into bed wearing his pajamas with boats all over them.

"But we can't have a boat right now," his mother reminded him.

With the innocence of a five-year-old, Joe suggested, "We could find one. Please take me out to Salt Fork Lake to see the boats."

It was difficult to resist Joe when he got a notion in his head. Just two years ago, Joe's adventuresome spirit had him starting up the outside ladder on their forty-foot silo one afternoon while Mom was fixing supper. He had been playing in the sandbox in the backyard when, quick as a wink, he was climbing.

Mom rushed outside but didn't want to yell at Joe, being afraid she would scare him. But his foot slipped and down he fell. This resulted in a serious injury that had him unconscious for two weeks. The doctors gave them little hope of Joe's complete recovery.

Then one day, Joe blinked his eyes and whispered, "I'll be okay."

Whatever happened during the time he was unconscious, Joe woke up a kinder young lad. He enjoyed helping his parents, teachers, and neighbors. Some said he was now a little angel.

So you can see why his thankful parents tried to give him things he wanted if at all possible, but a boat was not a possibility. However, they did agree to take Joe for a ride to Salt Fork Lake, where he could watch the boats at the Morning Glory boat ramp.

A picnic table in the shade of a tree provided the perfect place to spread out the food in their picnic basket and watch the boats drift by. Joe even went down to the edge of the lake and splashed in the shallow water. There were so many different kinds of boats that it was hard to pick a favorite. He even thought it would be great fun to water ski. "I wish we could have one of those boats," he told his parents.

Dad had recently been laid off from his job at the factory and they were struggling to make ends meet. Besides they were still paying doctor bills from Joe's extended hospital stay. A boat definitely did not fit in their budget right now.

But cheerful little Joe wasn't to be discouraged, "Someday I'll get a boat."

After they packed up their picnic supplies, Joe decided he would head back to the car by using a shortcut through a group of small trees. And there he spotted something on the ground—a billfold.

He rushed to his parents, excited as a pirate with a newfound treasure. "Look what I found!"

When Dad opened the billfold, he discovered four hundred dollars inside. *Wow, that would really help out with bills,* was the thought that ran through Dad's mind.

But Joe questioned, "Is there a name inside? I bet someone is upset that they lost it."

"Why, yes, Joe," Dad admitted. "It belongs to Gary Painter and it even has his address. Would you like to give it back to him?"

Remember, Joe always wanted to be helpful, so he anxiously agreed. He wasn't the least bit scared as he walked up to the door of Mr. Painter's house, which looked like a mansion in his eyes. Dad waited at the bottom of the steps.

A pleasant man with sparkling blue eyes answered the door. When Joe told him what he had found and where he had found it, Mr. Painter was ecstatic. Not only did it have four hundred dollars in it, but also his credit cards, extra keys, and some treasured pictures.

"Thank you, my boy," said the pleased gentleman as he hugged Joe. "Did you have fun at the lake?"

"Yes, sir. Someday I'm going to have a boat."

"Would you like to go for a boat ride?"

"Yes! Yes!" Joe jumped up and down, clapping his hands.

"Since you're such an honest young man, you can come ride on my boat any time you want." He handed the bouncing young boy a card with Mr. Painter's name and phone number. "Just give me a call, as I'm at the lake almost every weekend."

Joe smiled. It really was true that anything was possible. You just had to believe.

The Bouncers

BY JOY L. WILBERT ERSKINE

The wonders of weightlessness.

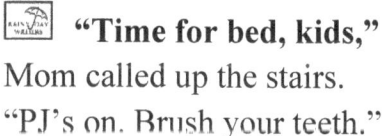 **"Time for bed, kids,"** Mom called up the stairs. "PJ's on. Brush your teeth."

"Oh, can't we play a little longer?" pleaded Arabelle, the oldest. "We'll be quiet. Won't we, kids?"

"We will, Momma," yelled Thomas, the second-oldest. Catherine, Edmund, and Lauren earnestly nodded assent.

"Get ready for bed and I'll give you another half-hour," Mom bargained.

"YAY!!" hollered the younger kids. "We can play!"

Arabelle shushed them. "Hurry, Thomas, you and Edmund brush your teeth. We girls will get our PJ's on. Then we'll switch."

Five little kids never moved so fast. Arabelle helped Lauren, inspecting quickly when everyone was done. "Good!" she pronounced. "Let's play!"

Five pairs of bare feet raced across the bedroom floor, leaping onto the huge iron four-poster bed where they slept together each night. Jumping up and down, they giggled with delight.

"Higher, higher," squealed Lauren, the youngest.

"Get on my shoulders," offered Thomas, kneeling on the bed. "Stop jumping, everyone. Let Lauren climb on." The others sat down, watching.

139

Lauren climbed fearlessly atop her brother's shoulders, stretching her three-year-old arms up. "Jump, Thomas. Me touch," she said, pointing.

"Not a good idea, Thomas," warned Arabelle. "If Lauren gets hurt, Mom's gonna be real mad."

"Oh…okay," Thomas agreed. "I'll just bounce a little. Wait, I know!" Dropping to his knees again, he slipped out from under Lauren's legs. "Watch me!"

Thomas climbed the bedpost with monkey feet and, stabilizing himself by touching the ceiling, crouch-walked to the middle of the headboard. Grinning, he dove feet-first to the middle of the bed, bouncing the others off their buns. Laughter filled the room as they toppled onto each other.

"Me too! I wanna jump!" giggled Catherine. Each took a turn climbing up, jumping gleefully onto the bed with a loud KA-whump.

"My turn! My turn!" Soon all five were atop the headboard, jumping. KA-whump! KA-whump! KA-whump!

"What on earth is going on up here?" asked Mom, coming through the bedroom door. Her mouth opened into an O. Her eyes got big as silver dollars. "Get down from there RIGHT NOW," she squalled. Five pairs of obedient bare feet jumped. KA-WHUMP!

Mom screamed. "Not like that! Are you trying to kill yourselves?"

Not a child spoke. Wide-eyed, they waited for Mom's next words, quick in coming.

"LOOK at that ceiling!" she roared.

Five pairs of eyes rotated to where Mom pointed—handprints smudged above the headboard.

"Down off the bed and stand in line," Mom ordered.

Whimpering, five children did as they were told. "Don't be mad, Momma," pleaded Arabelle, tears streaking her cheeks.

Mom fiercely smacked bums down the line, three per kid. "Arabelle, you should've known better," she growled. And Arabelle got an extra swat.

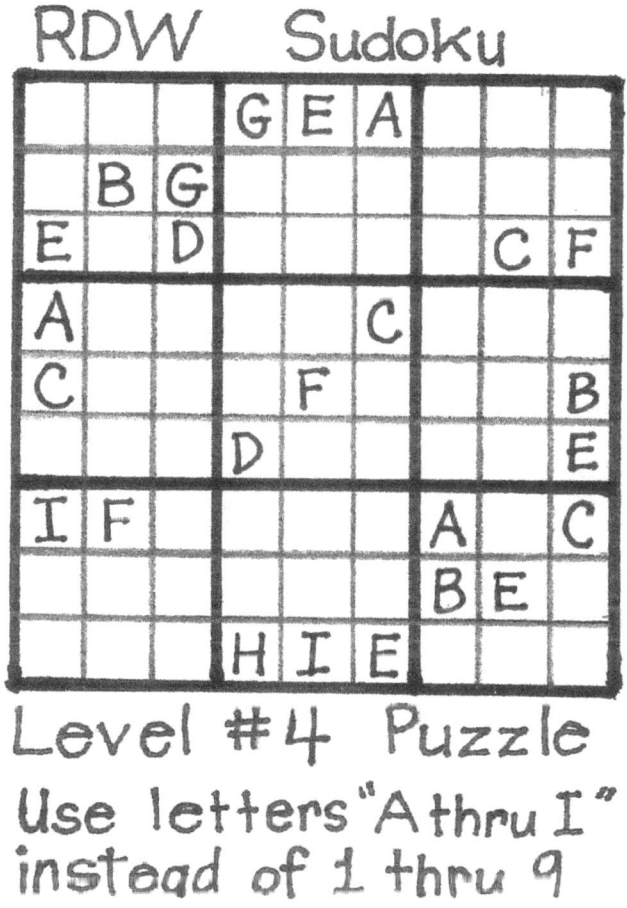

Level #4 Puzzle
Use letters "A thru I" instead of 1 thru 9

Solution on page 213.

The Break Up

BY MARTHA F. JAMAIL

Letting him down easy.

 Dear Writer's Block,

I knew someday I would have to write this letter and, in a way, I've always dreaded it. We've been together since fifth grade when I began the story "Once upon a time…" and suddenly you were there—shutting me out from further thought. I remember staring at those four words until the white paper almost blinded me. Your presence was so overwhelming that whenever I started to write, I could think of nothing else. You were still with me in eighth grade when I wrote, "It was a dark and stormy night…" and all I could think of was you.

I'm much older now and I realize we have quite a history together, but I must tell you something and, as usual, it is very difficult to say. Please know that I will always have a remembered past with you, but I think it is time for us to part ways. It's not you, it's me. I have needs now that you can't fulfill. I have story starters and deadlines to complete, and my eyes can no longer stare at the brightness of blank sheets of paper. And W.B., if I may call you that, and I say it fondly, I can no longer stay awake with you until the wee hours of the morning. I need my sleep and I need to be open to new ideas.

As you may have guessed, I have met someone else. I'll just call him M & I. He just came into my life one day out of nowhere. Actually, it was one night last year before the Christmas stories were due. M&I nudged me awake and walked me groggily to my computer. I sat in front of the screen and began to tap keys with abandon until an entire story was complete and ready to submit. You can imagine how thrilled I was because that had never happened before with you. I will always remember you and our times together, but I must say that M&I has to be my new companion.

I'm sure there are many writers out there who are already enjoying your company, so you'll never be alone. I'm sure we will continue to get together from time to time, but until then I wish you well.

Sincerely, Martha

P.S. M&I said you probably already know who he is—Memory & Inspiration.

Mystery solved

How many mystery writers does it take to change a light bulb? Two. One to screw the bulb almost all the way in and one to give it a surprising twist at the end.

FEATURE ARTICLE

Murder & Manhunt, 1865

BY RICK BOOTH

Take a step back into Guernsey County's interesting history.

A century and a half ago on a chilly Sunday evening, a man named John Gallup was calmly sitting in the kitchen of his Cambridge home, located near the site of today's Clark Street Circle K convenience store, when the distinctive crack of a gunshot startled him. Concerned, he rushed outside to the front gate of his property, looked about, and then heard the screams of a woman coming from several hundred yards away, somewhere toward the center of town. Quickly, he stepped back inside to grab his coat and hat, preparing to go see what was the matter. Walking fast towards town, he soon encountered two men trotting even faster on the same road, but heading in the opposite direction. Placing his hand on the shoulder of the taller of the two men, he asked if they knew what the commotion in Cambridge was about. "Some woman is making a fuss about something," the tall stranger replied as the two of them kept heading away from the scene.

John Gallup studied the two young men, thinking it strange that they would be rushing away from a woman's cries for help instead of toward them. Minutes later, he learned the truth and understood whom he had seen. Federal Provost Marshal John Cook, the local man charged with hunting down Civil War deserters, had just been murdered!

The Crime

Amarilla Cook, John Cook's wife and the mother of his six children, first met the tall stranger on Friday, March 3rd, 1865, two days before the shooting. He came to the family home, located on Wheeling Avenue just east of Eleventh Street, approximately where the parking lot of the Bundy-Law Funeral Home sits today. Introducing himself as a Mr. Smith, he asked if her husband was available. He said he wanted to report the whereabouts of a deserter. Amarilla explained that her husband was away on a short trip, but was expected to return by Sunday. The visitor turned and left.

This same tall stranger and his traveling companion had, in fact, been seen by many people in the Cambridge and Old Washington areas for several days before the shooting. No one knew their names. None knew from whence they had come.

On Sunday evening, the stranger returned to the Cook family home. Amarilla again answered the door and invited him in, explaining that her husband was just outside in the back yard. She called out to Mr. Cook, saying that he had a visitor, but he was slow to come in from outside. As the two waited the stranger made awkward small talk by inquiring of Mrs. Cook about where he could buy liquor in Cambridge. His breath already smelled of alcohol. Poor Mrs. Cook replied that she had little knowledge and no opinion on where to go drinking. She called for her husband again. At this, the stranger made excuse that he needed to check on his colt, which he said he'd left in the alley that ran along the east side of the house. He exited the front, walked along the alley to the back yard area, and, seeing a man in the yard, asked him if he'd noticed a wandering colt go by. He hadn't.

With at least one neighbor watching and listening to the transaction, the tall man asked, "Is your name 'Cook?'" When John Cook replied, "Yes," the man raised a revolver and fired. A single large bullet ripped into John Cook's chest. "Oh, what did you do that for?!" he exclaimed in his last conscious seconds before collapsing. Amarilla rushed into the darkened yard, found her husband bleeding and moaning on the ground, and screamed for help. It was not long in coming.

Within five minutes of the shooting, a doctor arrived. Cook was still alive, but life was ebbing fast. The physician and others carried the gravely wounded man into the house, where he died almost immediately. The bullet had pierced his heart.

Flashback

John Cook, had he not succumbed so quickly, might well have recalled a similar shot he took at a presumed fugitive one day in the summer of 1864. He had found a man thought to be a Union Army deserter at Gibson's Station, set along the B&O railroad line a few miles east of Lore City. The wanted man made a break for it when he realized he was about to be arrested. John Cook raised his gun and fired. But the bullet missed, and the fleeing man—a tall man—got away.

The Manhunt

John Gallup wasn't the only witness in town to notice two men fleeing the scene of the crime. Others had seen an accomplice, a second, shorter man, run north along Eleventh Street to join up with the killer in the Steubenville Avenue area. Together they rushed out of town along the Newcomerstown Road, which we now know as Clark Street.

A number of men immediately began searching for clues about the murder in the alley where the shooter had stood. Fortunately, the ground was wet, not frozen, and the murderer had left footprints. The footprints, in fact, were distinct, clear, and unique. The man in the alley had been wearing boots with unusually large metal plates attached at both toe and heel to prevent wear. At night, following the tracks was nearly impossible, but at first light on Monday morning the tracking party began its work.

The prints with the metal plates were found at Steubenville Avenue and along the Newcomerstown Road where John Gallup had met the strangers. The prints with metal plates were accompanied by a smaller man's footprints at their side. John's wife volunteered that she thought she had heard the men climb over the fence into the fields on the west side of the road. From there they could travel cross country. More prints were found in the field, along with a discarded empty whiskey bottle which 13-year-old Franklin Sipe identified as one he had sold to the shorter stranger the day before.

While some searchers scouted at rail stations, the tracking party, in fits and starts, followed the footprints for two days and many miles as they gradually meandered towards Birds Run in the northwestern part of the county. But by Tuesday evening, the trail had gone cold. The hunters had lost the tracks, given up, and turned back on their horses toward Cambridge. But just when it seemed that hopes of capture were lost, a quick-thinking woman outside Old Washington saved the day.

Miss Sarah Skinner was minding her business at home on Tuesday evening when a stranger appeared at the door. "Oh! I thought you was the man that killed Cook," she exclaimed. The man replied, "No, I am with the crowd who are searching for the men that did kill Cook. Is he dead?"

It shocked Sarah that the stranger did not know John Cook had died. Everyone had known that he was stone cold dead ten minutes after the attack! The man made the excuse that his search party had set out from Cambridge so quickly that he hadn't yet gotten word of Cook's fate. But that really didn't make sense to Sarah. The man had stopped, he said, because he was hungry and wanted to buy some food from her. She said she wouldn't part with the dried beef hanging over the mantle that he asked for, but she did sell him some small "light cakes" for about five cents each, totaling 85 cents. He wrapped the cakes in a noticeably dirty handkerchief before leaving. As he went back to the road in front of her house, she noticed another taller man join him. Having been asked by the stranger which way to go to get to the National Road turnpike, she then saw the men take off in a different direction. They ignored her as she called out that they were going the wrong way.

Sarah was sure these two must have been the wanted men. When they were out of sight, she grabbed her cloak and bonnet and set off for Old Washington to raise the alarm. At nearly the same instant, the dispirited tracking party that gave up near Birds Run was ambling back into Cambridge. They were soon to be granted new life.

News spread quickly, and a party of men returned to Sarah's house. They immediately found the footprints with the telltale metal plates. By then it was night, but at first light the tracking resumed. The fugitives were headed northeast. Finding a footprint here and there, the trackers covered nearly ten miles on Wednesday, ending that day's hunt just short of Londonderry in the far northeast corner of Guernsey County.

Captured!

Near midday on Thursday the tracking party took a meal at Edward Carpenter's farm at the west edge of the little town of Londonderry. While there, someone suggested they search Mr. Carpenter's barn which was set in a rather remote spot off the Cadiz Road, now known as State Route 22. Two men, George Washington Burson and Jesse Cook (of no known relation to the deceased John Cook), checked the interior of the barn while others hunted for the trail of the tracks nearby. Jesse Cook examined one side of the barn's interior, which contained a mowing machine and stacked sheaves of wheat. Burson checked the large pile of oat straw in the mow on the opposite side, using a pitchfork to shuffle it around. Cook shortly joined in that effort. Suddenly, a swipe of the pitchfork clearly revealed the shoulder of a man hiding under the pile. Immediately, Burson and Cook looked at each other and agreed out loud in their best acting voices that there was *"No one in the barn!"*

The two hunters then exited, closed the barn door, and shouted to the other distant members of their search party that there was *"No one in the barn!"* Their actions, however, spoke otherwise as they gestured frantically for all to come quick and assemble. When nine armed searchers had gathered and dismounted, Cook threw open the barn door and told them all to draw their guns. Then, for several tense minutes, men with nine loaded firearms were locked in a silent standoff with a pile of straw. Five times the call went out for the men hiding in the mow to come out and surrender. On the last call, it was announced that no more warnings would be given as the posse was preparing to riddle the mow with bullets. Only then did two sullen men emerge from the pile. Asked for their names, one man identified himself as John Wesley Hartup. The taller of the two said he was Hiram Oliver. At last, the prey had been caught!

One of the first orders of business with the captured pair was the examination of their footwear. Hartup's boots had no plates, but Oliver's were plated, toe and heel. They matched exactly the tracks the searchers had been following for four days! A further search of the mow turned up two fine, fully loaded Navy-issue revolvers. Then, when one of the members of the tracking party accused Hartup of murdering John Cook, he replied, "I didn't shoot him, but am with the man who did." He nodded his head toward Oliver, saying, "He can speak for himself."

The prisoners were bound up but otherwise were not threatened or subjected to any "barnyard justice," even though they literally were in a barnyard. On the way back to Cambridge, the entire party stopped to eat, and Hartup and Oliver wolfed at their food like men famished for days, which they no doubt were. When the party reached Old Washington, the telegrapher there relayed advance word to Cambridge that the hunted men had been caught and would arrive in town later in the evening. Word spread from one excited citizen to another in Cambridge until a significant gathering of curious spectators lined Wheeling Avenue, awaiting the return of the suspects.

A chillingly poetic passage in the Jeffersonian newspaper described the prisoners' return this way:

"At ten o'clock they came, guarded by about twenty men on horseback. When near the Court House the company commenced to trot down the street, followed by a large crowd of men and boys. A good deal of snow had fallen, and the men and horses were clothed in white from head to foot. The snow muffled the sound of the horses' feet, and not a word was spoken by the riders. It required no effort to the imagination to clothe them with spiritual garments and to fancy that a troop of spectres was passing by."

The horsemen dismounted in front of the Eagle Hotel on Wheeling Avenue between Sixth and Seventh Streets, on the site where the Penny Court building stands today. And from there it was off to the courthouse and jail.

The Winds of War and History

Hartup and Oliver were quickly indicted by a grand jury. For more than two months, they languished at the Guernsey County Jail in a building that once stood just behind today's courthouse in the area where a parking lot now separates it from the Guernsey County Public Library. The Guernsey County Prosecutor, Attorney Joseph D. Taylor, was out of state in Indiana, serving as Captain Joseph D. Taylor in a U.S. Army military legal affairs unit. It was expected that he would take a short leave to return to Guernsey County and prosecute the alleged murderers in Common Pleas court. The trial, some thought, should take about a week. But then events and the tides of history overtook the case and changed everything.

One month to the day after the ghostly riders brought Oliver and Hartup to jail, General Robert E. Lee surrendered his army to General Ulysses S. Grant at Appomattox Courthouse. The Civil War was all but over. The nation was jubilant. Five days later, President Lincoln was shot at Ford's Theater in Washington, D.C. He died the next morning. The nation was devastated. The ensuing successful days-long hunt for Lincoln's assassin eerily paralleled the successful days-long hunt for John Cook's assassin at Cambridge the month before. Distrust towards those not loyal to the Union cause escalated. The national mood shifted toward swift and angry calls for justice. Lincoln's death would be avenged. So, too, would be John Cook's.

When no trial in Cambridge had started for two months, people began to worry about the possibility of a jail break. Many said the guards were lax, and the Jeffersonian labeled the sheriff an outright incompetent. Informed of concerns that the prisoners could escape, on May 15th, Ohio's Governor John Brough sent seven soldiers to Cambridge to reinforce jail security. That same night, the Cambridge City Council met and adopted a resolution thanking the governor for the soldiers and intimating that another seven would gladly be received if he would like to send even more security to town!

Lincoln's assassination and the conspiracy behind it were initially regarded as crimes falling under civilian courts' authority. But on May 1st, 1865, President Andrew Johnson ordered that all conspirators should be tried by a military commission, despite the fact that none of them were serving in the military at the time of their crimes. Legal arguments involving martial law, time of war, and the president's position as military Commander in Chief were used to justify the switch from a civilian to a military court. There was a considerable amount of concern expressed publicly that the military court was simply chosen to ensure conviction, the arguments for removing it from civilian control being nothing but a bunch of legal sophistry. Nevertheless, the presidential decision was not reversed, and, on May 12th, testimony in the Lincoln conspirators' trial began in a military courtroom.

The events surrounding the Lincoln conspirators' trial no doubt helped charge the atmosphere in Cambridge for the thunderbolt of news that arrived on May 26th. On that day, a military commission was sent to Cambridge by General Joseph Hooker, regional commander of the war's Northern Department. They were sent to replace the civilian court's control of the Cook assassination case. By virtue of Cook's federally-authorized position as a provost marshal hunting down military deserters, an argument parallel to the one made in Washington was advanced to justify military control. And, as with the Lincoln conspirators, the expectation hung in the air that a military trial ensured conviction and harsh punishment.

A second bit of news about the commission convinced many in the Guernsey County community that the trial might be held with bias. Most of the military commission members were sent from Indiana, and the man charged with conducting the trial was none other than Judge Advocate Joseph D. Taylor, Guernsey County's prosecuting attorney who had been preparing from a distance to argue the case against Hartup and Oliver in Common Pleas Court!

The Military Trial

Before there was a beautiful Carnegie Public Library built on the Steubenville Avenue side of Guernsey County's courthouse square, the Cambridge Town Hall sat there. That is where, within a week of the announcement that the military commission would take over the case of Oliver and Hartup, the trial began. It was national news. It would also prove to be a trial like no other that Cambridge had ever seen.

Week after week, for nearly three months, witnesses were called. Some were local. Others traveled from as far away as Illinois to the west and a variety of states to the east. When it was over, the Cambridge community was very tired of the expensive spectacle, but at least it could be said that a very full picture of the Cook assassination and the perpetrators' motives behind it emerged.

The Jeffersonian, Guernsey County's

Democrat-run newspaper, was very critical of the conduct of the trial throughout, having opposed the decision to impose a military court from the start. The July 7th hanging of the questionably guilty Mary Surratt as a Lincoln co-conspirator—a woman regarded by many as nothing more than an innocent symbolic stand-in for her fugitive conspirator son John—further inflamed the Jeffersonian against the local military trial, which seemed a sure bet to find for the gallows. The competing Republican-run Guernsey Times newspaper, however, was supportive of the military commission and the general conduct of the trial. It saw no impropriety at all. Of course, it just so happened that the Guernsey Times newspaper was also owned by Guernsey County's prosecuting attorney, Judge Advocate Joseph D. Taylor. This is actual history! And no, you can't make this stuff up! The trial went on.

Testimony and evidence established that Hiram Oliver and John Hartup were brothers-in-law. Oliver was married to Hartup's sister, whose family then resided somewhere in the vicinity of Bloomfield, a few miles west of Cambridge. Hartup was unmarried, but Oliver had two children: a four-year-old daughter and an infant son.

Both Hartup and Oliver were about age 24. They had grown up and lived near each other in Jefferson County, Ohio, near Steubenville, before the war. Both had had trouble with the law, but both had also enlisted in Company A of the 43rd Ohio Volunteer Infantry in October, 1861. Oliver was discharged on a surgeon's certificate of disability the following July, and it is not entirely clear that he himself was a deserter, though he may have gone "absent without leave" (AWOL) for a time in the middle of his nine months of enlistment. Hartup, on the other hand, actually made a career out of deserting. He was what they called a "bounty jumper." Men were incentivized to volunteer for the army by promising a handsome up-front cash payment upon enlisting. Some would take the money, desert, and then reenlist elsewhere with a different unit for another bounty payment, often under a different name. Unless caught, it was a good way for unscrupulous individuals to build up a nice financial nest egg. Hartup had "jumped bounty" at least twice.

Hartup was also wanted for having stolen a large quantity of wool in the Steubenville area. He had once also boasted of shooting a man in Indiana. Oliver, likewise, had bragged to others that he was part of a widespread counterfeiting ring that was based in Wheeling, West Virginia. He claimed they produced very convincing "greenback" currency. To avoid the law, Oliver and Hartup had both moved to farms that they purchased near each other in Illinois, but social and perhaps criminal connections occasionally caused them to travel back to Ohio, regardless of their "wanted" status. It may have been on one such trip that Oliver encountered Provost Marshal Cook at Gibson's Station in the summer of 1864. Cook got off his one shot at Oliver, but failed to apprehend him. That encounter enraged Oliver, and he swore vengeance against Cook that many others who knew him—especially his acquaintances in Illinois—attested to. He told quite a few people that Cook had shot at him, and he hoped to return the favor someday. Oliver alleged that Cook had a reputation for jailing innocent men—or at least men who were, if not "innocent," at least not technically guilty of desertion.

Hiram Oliver had gotten wind that John Cook had discovered where he lived in Illinois and was likely to soon travel there to arrest him. He told others that if Cook did that, the sure result would be that one or the other of them would die. Not, therefore, intending to be the one who died, Oliver determined to travel to John Cook's home in Ohio and strike first. If he got away clean, he could live in peace on his Illinois farm. Oliver brought Hartup along on the assassination road trip to serve as his assistant!

Neither Hartup nor Oliver were Southern sympathizers. All testimony indicated they were loyal to the Union cause, albeit not quite above counterfeiting its greenbacks or taking its money in lump sums as often as possible by enlisting in the Union Army and then deserting. The assassination of Cook, unlike the Lincoln conspirators' parallel assassination, had nothing to do with the politics of North and South. It was a personal vendetta acted out by a scoundrel once targeted and shot at by John Cook at a small B&O rail stop in Richland Township, just a couple of miles east of Lore City.

Neither Oliver nor Hartup admitted guilt during the trial, though the evidence against them was utterly overwhelming. Witnesses, footprints, and boots clearly identified Oliver as the gunman and Hartup as his willing accomplice. A rather pathetic attempt to establish a time-of-the-crime alibi for the men was made using a female acquaintance's diary entries and a letter with a questionable postmark. Both items had been shown in evidence to try to establish that the men could not have been in Cambridge at the time of the murder. The ruse was transparent and did not work.

On August 10th, Judge Advocate Taylor received orders to transfer Oliver and Hartup to military Camp Chase in Columbus as soon as the hearings concluded. Accordingly, the trial ended with the transfer of the two prisoners to the state capital on August 30th while the verdict and sentence were still being deliberated by the military commission members. Hartup and Oliver were reportedly seen to be cautiously optimistic of some degree of leniency as they took the train west to await their fate.

Verdict and Execution

The wishful thinking of Oliver and Hartup came to an abrupt end on September 6th when the verdict and the sentence were read to them. Hartup was judged to be as guilty of murder in his capacity of accessory as Oliver was himself. Both men were sentenced to death. They were given 24 hours to brace themselves for their hangings in Prison Yard No. 1, which had been emptied of Confederate POWs between the time of their crime and their sentencing. The Civil War had ended in the interim.

Both men took the news hard, but Hiram Oliver had the most to come to terms with. Hartup grieved alone, but Oliver was allowed a last visit with his wife and children that same day at a camp guard house. A reporter sent by the Jeffersonian newspaper witnessed the scene and reported back to Cambridge the following graphic description.

"It was ours to view a most affecting scene—the parting between Oliver and his family. The man, dressed as we have described, was seated in the guard room, handcuffed, and with a ball and chain to his feet. By his side, with babe in her arms, was his wife, half crazed by grief and giving way to its most heart-rending expressions. The little girl, with wonder-struck face, stood near, gazing alternately at the soldiers with bayonets and her weeping parents. Reverends Vananda, of Columbus, and Ellison, of Cambridge, were both in attendance, and the officers and soldiers on duty completed the group. Both wife and husband exhibited much feeling, and their half-incoherent expressions of grief were painfully affecting to spectators. Several times came the firm, sorrowful order to go, but each time came such floods of bursting sorrow that the departure was delayed. And when at last the parting came—when he called his children to him, kissed them, and asked the blessings of God upon them, and turned to his wife with repeated farewells and earnest kisses, there was scarcely a dry eye in the assemblage. A sturdy soldier took the little girl in his arms, an officer supported the half-crazed mother to the door, and Oliver was alone with his clergymen."

The next day, shortly before the walk to the gallows, Oliver decided to confess. He admitted what had been made clear at the trial, including the fact that he was the gunman and Hartup was not. He expressed remorse for the harm he'd done to John Cook's family, his wife and his children. He also clarified and confirmed the presumed motive for the murder, with special emphasis on his wish to return a gunshot at John Cook after the 1864 incident at Gibson's Station. Indeed, he'd been remarkably accurate with his Navy-issue revolver, fired in the evening dusk from a distance of thirty to fifty feet, and yet striking Cook straight through the heart.

At one o'clock, a company of soldiers from the 22nd Veteran Reserve Corps formed a hollow square formation around the doomed men and the ministers assigned to accompany them. A military band played the Dead March as the procession moved toward the scaffold.

The Jeffersonian reported, "Scarcely was a start made when Mrs. Oliver, with heart-rending shrieks, broke away from her attendants and rushed with her babe toward her husband. Kindly but firmly she was restrained, and by those with tearful eyes taken to a more distant house and placed for a time under guard. Slowly, the funeral procession of men yet living moved on to the last dread scene in the terrible drama."

The two doomed men, dressed in black gowns, ascended the gallows. Prayers were offered by the clergymen, and then the men were allowed to speak their last words to the assembled audience of several hundred soldiers and civilian spectators. Oliver spoke first, confessing his crime, warning others to learn from his poor example, and further explaining he'd gotten religion in the past day with counseling by the ministers. In a firm voice, he said he felt he'd received God's forgiveness. He hoped to see all who were present someday again in heaven.

Hartup spoke in much the same vein, but his words were harder to hear as he struggled with his emotions. Black caps were then lowered over the faces of both men. Reverend Vananda offered a final short, eloquent prayer. At his closing 'Amen,' the trap was sprung. Hartup and Oliver died quickly, the only men ever executed at Camp Chase. Their bodies were cut down within the hour. Placed in two red coffins at the base of the scaffold, their mortal remains were offered to their families for burial.

Epilogue

Eight days after the executions of Oliver and Hartup, Captain Joseph D. Taylor received his discharge from the army. He left with an honorary "brevet rank" of colonel, an award entitling him to put "Col." before his name for the rest of his life, though he had only commanded men in a captain's capacity. The next year he married a young woman from a wealthy Quaker family in Maine whom he had met in Cincinnati during the war. He sold his interest in the Guernsey Times newspaper to relatives and practiced law in Cambridge while investing in many a business venture, some likely bankrolled by the in-laws in Maine. He built the Berwick

Hotel in Cambridge, as well as the large office building at the eastern end of the same Wheeling Avenue block. His beautiful Victorian mansion on Upland Avenue survives to this day as the Colonel Taylor Inn, a highly regarded bed and breakfast house. He served several terms in the U.S. Congress and was known as a friend of Presidents. From the end of the Civil War to his death in 1899, he bestrode Guernsey County like a colossus.

Amarilla Cook raised her children in Cambridge without a father, dying as an unmarried widow 28 years later in 1893.

Little is known of the subsequent fates of the other less-than-personally-famous players in the sad Cook murder drama. How poor Mrs. Oliver, who lost both husband and brother at a stroke, rebuilt her life is unknown, as are the later lives of her children.

Camp Chase was literally in the midst of being dismantled when the order came to hang two last men for murder. The old camp was soon lost under the post-war expansion of Columbus. The only remnant left today is a walled cemetery of Confederate dead from the Camp Chase prison, interred there by necessity.

The courthouse in Cambridge was torn down and replaced 16 years after the war. The jail and old town hall vanished, too.

Poignantly, the day before John Cook died in his own back yard, President Lincoln delivered his second inaugural address. It was reported word for word in the very same March 10, 1865, issue of the Guernsey Jeffersonian newspaper that announced the death of Cook. Lincoln's speech concluded, "With malice toward none, with charity for all, with firmness in the right as God gives us to see the right, let us strive on to finish the work we are in, to bind up the nation's wounds, to care for him who shall have borne the battle and for his widow and his orphan, to do all which may achieve and cherish a just and lasting peace among ourselves and with all nations."

Six months, two assassinations, one fatal manhunt, two military trials, and six executions later, Lincoln, Cook, and their respective assassins and co-conspirators all were dead. To Guernsey County, the time to bind up wounds had finally come. At last, the Civil War was over.

Everyone's got an opinion

In a college history class, the discussion was about the requirements to hold the office of President of the United States. The professor mentioned only two: A candidate must be 35 years of age and must be a natural-born citizen.

After a brief discussion, a student voiced an objection. "I don't think it's fair to limit it to being a natural born citizen. After all, a person born by Caesarian section would be just as capable!"
And, yes, they can vote!

RETROSPECTIVE

ret•ro•spec•tive (rĕt′rə-spĕk′tiv) *adj.* **1.** Directed to or retrospecting the past. **2.** Looking or directed backward. **3.** Applying to or influencing the past; retroactive. **4.** Of, relating to, or being a retrospective: *a retrospective exhibition. n.* An exhibition or performance of works produced by an artist over a considerable period. —**ret′ro•spec′tive•ly** *adv. Syn:* deliberative, absorbed, pensive, thoughtful.

Entering the Work Force

BY HARRIETTE MCBRIDE ORR

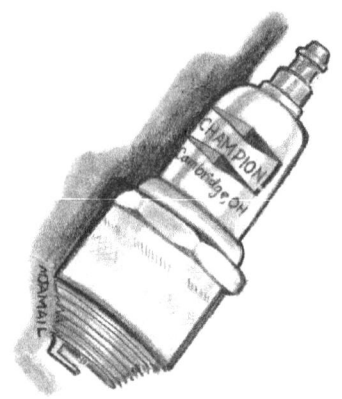

The greatest job I never wanted.

The first job I ever had was back in the late 1950s for S.S. Kresge's, the dime store, selling hardware, window blinds, gold fish, and turtles. Quite the combination.

From there, I went to Morton's Hat and Dress Shop on Wheeling Avenue in Cambridge, working for Grace Byers. Here, I became friends with her daughter Barb. She had recently applied for work at Champion Spark Plug and urged me to put my application in.

This I finally did with great apprehension. Did I really want to work in a factory? The salary and benefits were very attractive. I had a family to support, and my dream of a college education so I could teach school was not a possibility with three toddlers to raise.

One day Mrs. Byers informed me that detectives for Champion had been around checking on my work record. Soon after that, I was called to the plant for an interview. They had several of us come in to take a written test. We were told to make a decision, yes or no, when it came to the answers, not to put anything in the undecided column. Those who did not follow directions and placed their answers in the undecided column were not hired.

We were then called back to tell us we had been hired and were given a spark plug pin with our identification number. This we were to carry at all times.

We were taken on a tour of the plant. It was pointed out that women were expected to wear skirts or dresses. There were only one or two who wore pants and they were not looked on with favor.

There were men's jobs and women's jobs. When a job opening came up, you could bid on the job maybe in a different department or on a different shift. Whoever had the most seniority, got the bid. You had to be there a lifetime to get a day shift job.

We were told to report for work at 3 p.m. on Monday. That first day of work we "new hires" waited in the lunchroom until the foreman came for us. I was frightened to death. We were each assigned to stand behind an operator and watch how they worked till the bell rang for break time. Then the foreman, Tom J., took us each to a machine on the turning line. The machine I was assigned happened to be right across from my friend Barb, so I did feel better. I was designated a "turn and tip operator."

Spark plugs were formed on a huge press. Ceramic dust was fed down into the presses and into forms that produced a cylinder shape, known as a blank, with threads inside. These were lifted off the conveyor belt with a suction wand and placed into a wooden box. Layers were separated by cardboard. The boxes were then lifted onto wooden pallets and loaded as needed onto the turning line.

At the turning wheel, I was shown how to pick up four plugs at a time with my left hand and feed them onto a moving wheel, which held eight spindles. You had to be extremely careful not to bump the threads. Each plug went down and around, hitting a stone wheel which turned it, cutting the shape desired. As you fed the wheel with your left hand, at the same time you removed a plug with your right hand. The plugs were taken off the wheel one at a time, held over an air jet to blow out all the dust, and placed into a round stone container called a sagger, which was on a turntable. The plugs were stood up, perfectly straight, one in front of the other. The last item inserted was a ceramic cup with your number inside. Then packing material was stuffed around the cup with a wooden pick to make them snug so when picked up and placed on the kiln cars they wouldn't move. The material handler punched your card for every sagger he picked up.

It was a long first day. The noise and confinement were overwhelming.

Thirty saggers a shift was the expected rate, depending on the size of the plug. We had thirty days to make our rate. Being left handed was not to my advantage. When the work buzzer rang, you turned your machine on, and when it rang again, you shut it off. We had two ten minute breaks and a half hour for lunch. I felt like I was in prison.

When the stonecutting wheel became dull, the plugs would burst and spray dust and material all over you, usually in your face. We had a light to put on to summon the setup man. He would eventually come down and sharpen your wheel, writing down time on your card, meaning you did not have to make plugs for the time he worked on your machine.

Inspectors came around and took eight of your plugs and checked them out several times during a shift, making sure they were being turned to the right size.

A small paint brush was provided so you could keep your wheel spindles clean and brush any junk material down a hole to be reused. A tiny fan was positioned above your head to supposedly cool you.

What a relief when the final bell rang at 11:00 p.m. and we were out the door, headed home.

With the help and encouragement of the seasoned workers, I finally made rate before my thirty day probation was up and became a member of The United Auto Workers, as was required.

As time went on, I became a skilled worker and ended up changing shifts to work third or midnight shift. I also was the union steward on my shift, representing any worker called into the office for a work related problem. This I did for twenty some years.

I gave my best to Champion and ended up retired at the age of fifty two.

"Bloom where you are planted" is my mantra. Factory work was not what I had envisioned for my life, but it worked out to be an okay thing. Thank you, Champion Spark Plug.

Time will always tell

I can't believe I got fired from the calendar factory. All I did was take a day off.

Prices

BY BOB LEY

Generational economics, plus interest.

People my age...not quite four score (do you remember how old that is?)...purchased gasoline at around seventeen cents per gallon at the height of the "gas wars" among filling stations. We also got the oil checked and the windshield washed. Many stations could service your car too!

My stamp collection as a boy consisted primarily of versions of the three cent stamp. That was the going price of mailing a letter then. The penny postcard was usually pre-printed with a one cent stamp.

Interest at most banks was three percent paid on your savings account, while often loans were at six percent. The difference was what kept most banks afloat then.

I found one of Dad's old budget books not long ago. The year was 1941. He was making fourteen dollars a week. Inside the ledger was a grocery shopping list. Bread was eight cents a loaf. Milk was fifty-four cents a gallon and delivered to your house.

Twenty two years later, in 1963, I made sixty five dollars a week and drove a new car. Okay, it was a four door Corvair, not exactly a "babe wagon," but it *was* new!

The most frightening money issue happened to me in 1956. My dad owned a menswear store. He had worked long hours and put everything he had into it, to make it successful. The store was his lifelong dream.

One evening he came home from work looking morose. Since that was not his usual attitude, we steered clear, waiting for him to be ready to tell us what happened. We all were imagining the worst!

Finally at dinner, Mom broached the subject. "It can't be anything we can't solve together. What's the problem?"

The color had drained from his face. He looked at all of us and said, "H.L. Hartz (his main suit supplier) raised the prices on their suits again. I just can't absorb another price increase." His pain was very real. "I have to raise the price of suits from thirty-nine dollars to $42.50. I'm afraid that'll be the end of the men's suit business. It's hard enough to ask a man for thirty nine dollars. Nobody will pay forty two fifty for a suit!"

He looked around the table. "If that happens, we'll probably have to close the store." For the first time in my life, I saw my Dad near tears.

Of course closing the store didn't occur, but we spent a scary few months waiting to see what happened.

Today there seems to be no limit on prices. I see suits advertised from six hundred to twelve hundred dollars and apparently they sell.

The financial picture has evolved during my lifetime and like most of my generation, I fear for the younger ones coming into adulthood. When I graduated high school, the Dow Jones was around 650. Today, even after several tough years, it is triple that. I am sure they'll be just fine.

Home Schooling 101

APPRECIATION OF A JOB WELL DONE:
"If you're going to kill each other, do it outside! I just finished cleaning."
RELIGION:
"You better pray that comes out of the carpet."
TIME TRAVEL:
"Behave, or I'll knock you into the middle of next week!"
LOGIC:
"Because I said so. That's why."
FORESIGHT:
"Make sure you put on clean underwear, in case you're in an accident."
IRONY:
"Keep crying and I'll give you something to cry about!"
OSMOSIS:
"Shut your mouth and eat your supper."
CONTORTIONISM:
"Just look at the dirt on the back of your neck!"
STAMINA:
"You'll sit there until that spinach is gone."
HYPOCRISY:
"If I've told you once, I've told you a million times. Don't exaggerate."

It's About Time

BY DONNA J. LAKE SHAFER

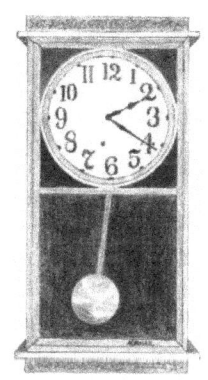

Sometimes life gets a little off kilter.

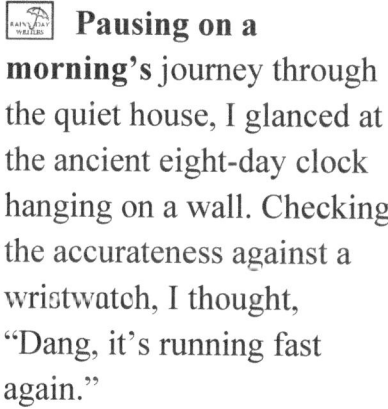 **Pausing on a morning's** journey through the quiet house, I glanced at the ancient eight-day clock hanging on a wall. Checking the accurateness against a wristwatch, I thought, "Dang, it's running fast again."

My thoughts went back to the first time I saw that old clock. It was in the basement of my childhood home. Dad had retrieved it from the remains of a barn that was about to be razed. Its original home had probably been a schoolroom or maybe a train depot. Dad soon learned that in its present condition it was inoperable. No matter. He knew just the fella who could diagnose and repair the timepiece.

In a short time, the clock, now performing well but still rather ugly except for the new face, graced the wall of what we called "Daddy's Hole." There was a pot-bellied stove, a couple old but comfortable chairs, and an ancient kitchen cabinet which held a collection of hand tools and other treasures. There were also books, mostly Zane Grey novels, Dad's favorite. This space today would probably be called a "Man Cave." It was a great place for dad-daughter chats even in later years, as well as a reclusive area for some quiet time for him.

When I was grown and had a home of my own, I became more interested in the old clock. On close inspection, it was evident that under many layers of paint, there seemed to be some decorative carvings at the top and bottom. Fascinated, I was soon coveting the thing and imagined it restored to its original beauty and hanging in a strategic spot in my own house.

Finally, after sensing my growing obsession, Dad presented the clock to me along with his old violin. He had had the instrument for many years. We had both played; he pretty good, me rather badly. It might have helped if either of us could read music, but we were both "play by ear" types.

On gaining possession of both treasures, my first order of business was to strip the clock of the ancient cracked paint. What a mess! A sewing needle was needed to delicately dig layers of the stuff out of the tiny grooves. But, when the handwork and beautiful oak wood were exposed, I knew my efforts were well worth it. It was soon hung and admired. Wound every eight days as it demands, it has faithfully kept correct time for me and my family for more than fifty years.

Until now.

Standing back and gazing at the relic, I could almost hear Dad's voice reminding of a very important feature of such a timepiece. "You must make sure it's hanging completely level. If not it will gain or lose time. Listen carefully. Hear it? It's saying TOCK-TICK instead of TICK-TOCK." Doing as he reminded me, I listened. Yes. It was definitely making the wrong sound.

Locating a household

level, I checked and corrected the slight imperfection. Winding it and giving the now sparkling brass pendulum a little shove, I carefully closed and latched the door. Then, standing back, I listened to the sound of that faithful old clock. TICK-TOCK, TICK-TOCK, TICK-TOCK.

Remembering again, a memory goes back to that time when Dad presented me with the clock and the old violin. He had placed a note in the bottom of the clock, where it still resides. Yellowed and brittle with age, it reads, "Hang up the clock; sit back and fiddle while time marches on. Guess Who?"

Home Schooling 102

CIRCLE OF LIFE:
"I brought you into this world and I can take you out."
ANTICIPATION:
"Just wait until we get home."
HUMOR:
"When that lawnmower cuts off your toes, don't come running to me."
GENETICS:
"You're just like your father!"
ROOTS:
"Shut the door! Do you think you were born in a barn?"
WISDOM:
"When you're my age, you'll understand."
JUSTICE:
"One day you'll have kids, and I hope they turn out just like you!"

Shortcut?

BY HARRIETTE MCBRIDE ORR

Dick was one lucky duck!

 The time was the mid-1950s, on a crisp sunny winter day. Dick and his friend were headed to the park to play some basketball. As they walked along Ninth Street, they decided to take a shortcut to the court by crossing the frozen Duck Pond.

As they neared the middle of the pond, they heard and felt a crack under their feet. The next thing they knew, the ice was giving way.

They took off running. Making it to shore, his friend turned around and Dick was nowhere to be seen. There was just a hole in the ice. Quickly, he ran to the neighbor's and they called the fire department.

Falling into the cold water, Dick was quickly dragged to the icy depths below. Fighting with all his might, he surfaced, only to find he was still under the ice. After several futile attempts, he found the hole in the ice and was able to get his head out of the water. Gasping for breath, he saw no one around. He hollered for help as he tried to pull himself out of the water by putting his leg up onto the ice. Time after time, he got that leg up, only to have the ice break away.

By the time the fire department arrived, Dick had

been in the water close to fifteen or twenty minutes. His strength was nearly gone. They tried throwing ropes to him and he was too weak to grab them.

They laid a ladder out onto the ice and one fireman crawled out the ladder, hoping to get the rope around Dick so they could pull him out. But the ice broke under him and the fireman found himself sinking. He now struggled for his own life as his heavy boots filled with water, dragging him under, with Dick hanging onto his neck. Finally, his boots came free and he was able to surface and grab the rope they threw to him.

By this time, Dick's strength was gone and he passed out. He didn't remember being pulled out of the water or being carried down the street to a neighbor's house, where he was put to bed with hot water bottles and piles of blankets to warm him.

Being a sixteen year old boy, he was thrilled to death when he finally woke up and realized he was in the home of one the most popular girls in high school and, lo and behold, was in her bed. This gave him something to brag about to the guys and helped ease the pain of falling through the ice. Today, Dick would have been whisked off to the hospital, not just taken to a neighbor's.

Looking back on this harrowing experience of sixty years ago, Dick said he later went back to the Duck Pond to check things out and found that he had been going around in circles trying to get out of the water. If he had gone in a straight line he would have made it to shore.

Dick never ventured out onto the frozen pond again. This was one shortcut he wished he had never taken. It turned out okay, with never any side effects. But be careful out there, and when you are tempted to take a shortcut maybe you should think twice. Sometimes, the long way around is the best way around.

Home Schooling 102

CIRCLE OF LIFE:
"I brought you into this world and I can take you out."
ANTICIPATION:
"Just wait until we get home."
HUMOR:
"When that lawnmower cuts off your toes, don't come running to me."
GENETICS:
"You're just like your father!"
ROOTS:
"Shut the door! Do you think you were born in a barn?"
WISDOM:
"When you're my age, you'll understand."
JUSTICE:
"One day you'll have kids, and I hope they turn out just like you!"

Family Life on the Ohio River

BY BEVERLY WENCEK KERR

Row, row, row your boat.

Watching the tugboats and barges drift down the swift Ohio River was as exciting a hundred years ago as it is today. Those who lived along its edge experienced pleasures and chores quite different from those who lived in the hills of Guernsey County.

While riding the Fly Ferry recently, Bud Price and his wife told about his life on the Ohio River from childhood to adult. His experiences have been recorded here...as best they can be remembered.

As a small child, Bud lived on the banks of the Ohio River just below Williamson Island, which is located north of Fly, Ohio, and Sistersville, West Virginia. Five sisters and four brothers formed this large family. Even though very poor, they never realized it.

Summer break from school consisted of at least four months so children could help their parents with planting and harvesting. Each member of the family had assigned chores daily. Only after finishing all their tasks could they enjoy playing at the water's edge.

Racing boats provided

hours of entertainment. Every family owned at least one row boat, usually a couple. With no bridges for miles in any direction, the rowboat became the only means of crossing the Ohio River at that time.

Often, the boys would race from the bank of the Ohio to Williamson Island and back again. Bud learned at an early age to paddle quickly. He could move the oars as fast and smoothly as the Indians that had lived there long before.

After racing, a hot summer day might end with a swim in the cool waters of the Ohio River. Throwing their overalls on the bank and stripping down to boxers or, most often, their birthday suits, the boys found this the perfect way to cool off at the end of the day. Racing was exhilarating, but not as satisfying as swimming.

But the river didn't only contain fun for the boys. Work always came first. Often their father would paddle a larger boat over to the island with all four brothers. Their job for the day was to gather coal from the edge of the island and pile it up on shore.

At that time, coal particles accumulated along the edges of the Ohio River banks and the banks of the islands as well. They appeared because of the area coal mining and washing along the banks over the years. Also, lumps of coal often fell from barges passing on both sides of the island. Not everyone could or would go to the island and get the coal that had been washed up there.

Dad would move the boat along the shore while the boys loaded the coal into the boat for him to take home. Due to the weight of the coal, their rowboats couldn't hold the coal and the boys. So the boys stayed on the island "picking coal" while, on the other end, the girls in the family helped unload the boat. Bud remembered holding the smooth lumps of coal after they had been tumbled in the river.

This important summer job filled the coal bins at home to use for winter heat. Their mom also needed it to heat her cook stove. That coal-fired stove provided good home-cooked meals, as well as a warm home. This Pennsylvania coal burned very well.

The children all helped with the large family garden on the bank of the Ohio River. Here, the rich soil produced a bounty of delicious produce. Planting, weeding, and harvesting vegetables kept everyone busy from May to September.

Mom and the girls sometimes spent all day canning green beans, corn, beets, peas, and carrots.

Most families had no refrigeration at that time and often kept things cool at the water's edge. Home freezers not being a possibility, the only way to keep vegetables through the winter was to can them or store some in their fruit cellar.

Even then, family and neighbors took time for fun and relaxation. Many evenings, they sat on the bank and watched the barges go by. Some evenings, a steamboat playing its calliope would entertain them as it slowly glided past.

Today, Bud and his wife still live high on a hill where they can watch the Ohio River flowing by. It holds many memories for them and they find it a peaceful place to live. Bud remarked, "There's always something to be thankful for." I imagine he's very thankful he doesn't have to row out to the island these days to "pick coal."

Sundays

BY BOB LEY

Oh, those wild weekends!

On Saturdays, my brothers and I cleaned our rooms and got a white shirt ironed for Church Sunday. We pulled a shirt—washed, starched and rolled—out of the refrigerator where they were kept damp until all were ironed.

My brothers and I became adept at having both our room cleaning and our ironing pass Mom's white glove inspection the first time. It's when I first heard the axiom: *It's quicker to do it right the first time!*

Sundays meant Church. We dressed in our best. Not necessarily top of the line, but always our best. Dad often said, "If you were invited to the White House, you'd undoubtedly get dressed up. Same thing goes for Our Lord's House." Afterward, we spent a few minutes milling around the church foyer, saying hello and "catching up."

Mom usually fixed roast chicken, varying it occasionally with a beef roast or a ham, depending on what Mr. Fitzgerald, our corner grocer, had on special. Since very few businesses were open on Sundays in those days, we had Dad to ourselves.

The "day of rest" for him meant relaxation, which is not always the same as restful. We took walks, stopping at various porches for brief conversations. We carved pumpkins in October. We made snow angels and snowmen in the winter.

Most Sundays, the phone would not ring all day (imagine!)...others were busy doing the same as we did.

Without fail, we capped our Sunday with *The Ozzie and Harriett Show* on the radio. Worn out from our "day of rest," we were often in bed before dark.

Seems like a boring existence by today's standards: meaning, sleeping in as long as you want. Cell phoning or texting a dozen or so of your closest friends. Watching TV all afternoon. Near dark, going out to meet some friends.

Once in a while, I wish I could share my version of a nice Sunday. Somehow, I don't imagine it would be met with much enthusiasm. Ah, well, I wouldn't trade those days for anything.

Sound advice

The secret of a good sermon is to have a good beginning and a good ending, and to have the two as close together as possible. –George Burns

Remember When

BY SAMUEL D. BESKET

It wasn't all that long ago...

 Remember when... everyone who owned a television had a large antenna mounted on a pole or strapped to their chimney? We only received two channels. They were in black and white and signed off playing the National Anthem at midnight.

Remember when... if you were sick, I mean really sick, the doctor came to your house, you didn't go to the doctor's office?

Remember when... someone in the family died, the body was returned to the home for visitation? A black wreath was placed on the front porch and people took turns sitting up with the deceased.

Remember when... a couple was married, kids in the neighborhood would "bell" them? Getting "belled," it was called. When the newlyweds returned home from their honeymoon, we would sneak up to the house and make a lot of noise with a bell, pan, or bucket until the groom came and gave us some candy or money.

Remember when... Routes 40 and 21 were the main highways through the county? Every fifty miles or so there was a roadside park where you could get a cool drink of water from a well or eat the lunch you packed before you left home.

Remember when… you pulled into a gas station and the attendant pumped your gas, checked your oil and cleaned your windshield? You "paid at the pump," only with cash…credit cards weren't around yet.

Remember when… in order to make a phone call, you first had to pick up the phone and listen to see if anyone was on the "party line?" Then you dialed zero for the operator and gave her the number you wished to call. The operator would ring the party for you.

Remember when… you didn't have to be an electrical engineer to know how to turn on the TV or make a phone call or a cup of coffee in the morning?

There is an old saying, "It's so easy to use, a six-year-old can do it." Now we need a six-year-old to program all our devices for us.

Remember when… we went outside to use the bathroom and stayed inside to eat, and *getting stoned* meant a kid threw stones in your yard?

Remember when… attending church on hot summer days before we had air conditioning, the only way to cool yourself was with the small fans found on the back of the pews? Usually, they were supplied by the local funeral home.

Remember when… you called a business or store and a real live person who spoke fluent English answered the phone? You didn't have to press four or five buttons only to get the voicemail of the person you wished to talk to.

Thrill of a Lifetime

BY HARRIETTE MCBRIDE ORR

Carnegie Hall calling. Can you hear me now?

How do you get to Carnegie Hall? "Practice, practice, practice" is the usual answer. Carnegie Hall in New York City is celebrating its 125th Anniversary in 2016. What exciting memories this brings to mind. Twenty-five years ago, I was privileged to sing at Carnegie Hall.

If you ask anyone who was a member of "The Cambridge Singers" of Cambridge, Ohio, in 1991, they can tell you it took not only practice, but lots of hard work and dedication to get forty people to New York for the weekend and learn the most difficult musical work we had ever attempted.

Our director, Mary Fran McClintock, had received three telephone calls from Carnegie Hall, which she thought were a joke. Finally, they got through to her that it was really Carnegie Hall calling to invite The Cambridge Singers to come to New York and be part of a large chorus to help celebrate the 100th birthday of the Hall.

A board meeting was called for June of 1990, where Mary Fran played the telephone message for us to hear. We were mesmerized and could not believe our ears. We were so excited.

Could it be that this chorus from Southeastern Ohio would be performing in Carnegie Hall? It is well known that performing at Carnegie Hall is a great honor and is not open to just anyone, so why did we receive this invitation?

Mary Fran learned that one of her fellow choral directors, John Drotleff, had heard us perform and had submitted our name to MidAmerica Productions, who handle the bookings for Carnegie Hall.

After looking over the performance dates offered, Mary Fran suggested we consider December 3rd. At that time, one of our favorite composers, John Rutter, who conducts the Cambridge Singers of Cambridge, England, would conduct.

A fundraising committee was organized and contributions to this fund came from many sources throughout the area. Our budget to get forty people to New York was $26,290. Yard sales were held and collections were taken at our spring and Christmas shows. Each member had to pay $150. No one was left behind.

On Thanksgiving morning November 28, 1991, at 8:00 a.m., we boarded a Kamm Tour bus headed for "The Big Apple." We stopped in Scranton, Pennsylvania, at Big Ed's Steakhouse for a traditional Thanksgiving turkey dinner. It was an emotional time for all of us. The excitement of the trip and the sadness of leaving family behind on this holiday presented a pot of mixed emotions.

By six thirty that evening, we got our first glimpse of the New York skyline. Our hotel was in midtown Manhattan, right across the street from Madison Square Garden. It was at one time the Hotel

Penta, from which Glenn Miller and the Pennsylvanians broadcast their radio show. Miller's composition, "Pennsylvania 6-5000," is the hotel's phone number still today. We found the hotel by no means modern, but it served the purpose.

As we checked in, we started to notice some strange characters roaming around. Ahead of us in line was none other than Chewbacca and, right beside him, a short little green Yoda. Standing near the elevators were storm troopers and Darth Vader himself. The hotel had been invaded by Star Wars characters, there for a convention.

At nine thirty Friday morning, there were over three hundred chorus members from all over the United States gathered in the hotel ballroom. We were briefed by Mr. Loy of MidAmerica Productions. He gave us instructions about the courtesies Mr. Rutter would expect. Mr. Rutter was introduced and our day of very exciting, intense work was begun.

Thanks to the knowledgeable interpretation of Mr. Rutter's music by our director, and the wonderful skill and talent of our accompanist, Mary Ann Rigel, The Singers had very little trouble following Mr. Rutter's direction of his wonderful "Magnificat."

During our short breaks, Mr. Rutter took time to talk and sign autographs for everyone. The Cambridge Singers presented him with a dozen of our show glasses with our Singers logo and the 1991 date engraved. He accepted them most graciously and said he was happy to meet "the other" Cambridge Singers.

At five p.m., we were free for the day. Some

people stayed close to the hotel; others had dinner reservations or were off to see the sights. A few had tickets for a Broadway play. Some shopped Macy's next door and then walked to the Empire State Building to see the wonder of New York at night.

Early Saturday morning, we boarded our bus for Carnegie Hall. We were the first to arrive, so we had plenty of time to see the outside, as well as the interior. Carnegie is a union hall, so we were not allowed to take pictures inside. We were thrilled to see the poster advertising our show listing, "The Cambridge Singers" of Ohio.

The outside of Carnegie Hall is very unimposing but, if you know the history of the hall, you realize its importance to the music world. Many musicians have obtained their start right there on its stage. The inside gives the impression of quiet elegance, with the acoustics being unmatched in the world. It was built for the small sum of two million dollars, donated by steel magnate Andrew Carnegie.

At one time, Carnegie Hall was threatened by the wrecking ball. It was through the endeavors of Isaac Stern that the state legislature of New York passed the Bard Act, enabling the city to purchase the building and lease it back to the Carnegie Foundation. In 1986, it was restored to its present splendor at the cost of 60 million dollars.

Walking on stage for the first time, I personally was overcome with a feeling of awe. There I was, standing on the stage where hundreds of world famous musicians have performed.

Soon the chorus members were lined up according to vocal section and height. The risers we were to stand on had just enough room for all of us to squeeze onto, with a metal frame on the ends to hold us in place. There was no room to move. One had to read the music of the person in front of you. Your own music, someone else read. If you suffered from claustrophobia this was no place for you.

When practice ended, we were transported to St. Bartholomew's Church, where, under the direction of Mary Fran, accompanied by Mary Ann, we sang several religious numbers.

Returning to our hotel, we met the AAA bus from Cambridge with thirty-nine fans, family, and friends aboard. My cousin, daughter, and best friend were among the new arrivals. We were so glad to see them. The evening was spent with the newcomers, having dinner and sightseeing, as well as shopping Fifth Avenue and riding a horse-drawn carriage around Central Park.

Sunday morning found us off to breakfast and church, stopping at FAO Schwartz Toy Store, The Trump Tower, and attending the glorious Radio City Music Hall's Christmas show.

At three p.m., we had our last practice at the hotel. We were joined by Melanie Marshall, an opera star from Great Britain. She had just arrived on the Concorde and was so pressed for time she sang with her coat on. Mr. Rutter had composed the song "Distant Land" just for her. That night would be its debut.

That evening we had a long wait at Carnegie, but we soon found ourselves filing on stage. We had time to check out the audience and found the many familiar faces of the sixty-some people who were there just to watch the Cambridge Singers.

The performance went well. The first thing we knew, it was over and we were headed upstairs to the top balcony to watch the rest of the show. After the show, we received accolades of praise from people on the street and our family and friends. We said goodbye to those from home as they boarded the bus headed back to Cambridge. They would travel all night.

By ten thirty, all of the chorus members were bused to Lincoln Harbor, where we boarded a tour boat for dinner and a water tour of New York at night. The boat was crowded, but there was plenty of champagne and lots of good music. The sights of New York were breathtaking.

At ten a.m. Monday morning, we were headed west toward home. It had been a wonderful experience. One we never shall forget.

As the bus traveled toward home, we began to come down from the emotional high we had maintained for several days. We returned to Cambridge in a downpour of rain and tears.

The Cambridge Singers had experienced something that very few people are ever privileged to do. New York was a wonderful time for all of us. This experience will remain in our hearts forever.

Happy Birthday, Carnegie Hall! May you celebrate many more years of wonderful music! How do you get there? "Practice. Practice. Practice."

The Lost Art

BY BOB LEY

Sept. 20, 2016
Dear Barbara,
What a lovely surprise I received in the mail today — a beautiful blue mosaic bowl from you! I placed it in the center of the dining table....

Ah, the joy, the feeling, the sincerity of a letter.

My mother and my wife were letter writers. They were real letters, with the address and date at top right, then the recipient's name and address below on the left as we learned in English class!

Their letters were elegant works of art. Even a simple thank you letter had excellent craftsmanship. The sincerity was demonstrated in the care in which it was written.

Due to her health, mother can no longer write. It has been a great sadness to her. I think she hated losing that ability more than giving up her driver's license. The correspondence she carried on provided a deep satisfaction. I know I miss seeing her letters in my mailbox. It is certain many others feel the same.

Today, e-mail and texting have practically replaced letters, especially social letters. They both offer speed, convenience, and immediacy; they sacrifice the vivid descriptive phrases which are the personality of a nicely written letter.

Words like "w8" (wait), "b4" (before), "2day" (today), and "LMAO" (phrase meaning funny) are commonly in use, along with thousands of others. More are added daily. I may have to read *English for Dummies* if I am going to converse with my grandchildren in particular, maybe even the world in general!

"C U latr" (See you later) somehow does not feel as personal as I would like. "LOL" (depending on context means Lots of Luck, Loads of Laughs, or one of several others) seems to be the most overused word in the e-lexicon.

A quote from one of my wife's old letters, *"I hope and pray for you the trip is all you dreamed of"* would make me feel she meant it more than "Gd luk w/trip."

With a cell phone in most every hand, even those of a very young age, often firmly planted to an ear, communication is more plentiful than ever in history, though its quality may be suspect. It seems few skills are being developed to have meaningful dialogue.

Talking to a grandchild who is having a surreptitious texting conversation with a friend (they can text without looking!) is not rewarding. More than once, I have ended a conversation early, saying, "We'll talk when you have time for me." They cannot figure out how we know. Some things never change! They like to think of it as multitasking. I think of it as rude.

Penmanship, an almost forgotten word, was a once-prized skill. I am sure it is still taught in schools, but most skills don't improve unless practiced. Do you remember the lessons in cursive writing that consisted of drawing continuous overlapping circles across the page, being careful not to go outside the lines? It did produce some proficiency.

Both my mother and my wife had exquisite handwriting. Mother's was more "Old World." It would remind one of the charts around a second grade classroom, showing the correct form for every letter. My wife's hand had more flourishes, but was well done and easy to read.

Even the stationery used was part of the effort. Notebook paper or a sheet of legal pad was never used. It simply didn't fit the kind of writers they both were.

I wonder when I see two teenagers, not fifteen feet apart, texting each other. It is obviously their choice for conversation. But will they be able to converse in the workplace, either vocally or with the written word? To be fair, all businesses today use computers and cell phones. Often a signature is all that is required, and many of those are difficult to decipher, but there are many situations that require a one-on-one conversation or a well-constructed letter to win a point.

People of my age are always lamenting change. It is difficult to give up things that meant something important to us. It is sad that many of the younger generation will never know the joy, the feeling, the sincerity of a letter. It is a lost art. In this new world of computers, laptops, notebooks, pads, and smart phones, I suppose we'll never go back to letter writing…but I miss it.

Progress!

A television can insult your intelligence, but nothing rubs it in like a computer.

The Summer of Deep Pond

BY BEVERLY WENCEK KERR

Sweet summer memories.

 "Let's go down to the stream in the woods."

"Want to play catch?"

"Race you on my bike to Granny's house."

Shouts like these echoed down the hallway when my sons rolled out of bed in the morning back in the 1970s. Today, you seldom see children playing outside and enjoying nature, but that wasn't the case with my two sons. They explored the woods and the world around them on a daily basis while growing up. The weather had to be pretty bad outside to keep them in the house.

When Gene was eleven and John was eight, they frequented the woods behind our house. At the edge of the woods, a beautiful waterfall plunged down the cliff for twenty feet. Water flowed rapidly from this spring-fed falls into a stream below.

This stream had their attention that summer as two large trees had fallen across the water below a small bend. Always thinking of something to create, John remarked, "Wonder if we could make a dam and have our own swimming pool?"

"Yeah, let's try it. Let's gather some things from the woods and see if we can fill in the holes between the trees." Gene couldn't wait to begin. They were determined to have a swimming pool. The only question was how deep could they make it?

Building a dam takes hard work. Every time water built up, some spot would break through. But both boys had patience, time, and a burning desire for a swimming pool. This wasn't their only summer fun, because they took breaks from dam building several times a week, when they headed to the baseball diamond for Gene's Little League practice or games.

The bed of the stream felt slick as slate. Often the bottom was so slippery that standing up became difficult. The water rushed down the stream rapidly on a daily basis, but after a rain the stream's added force made it difficult to stand.

Once started, nothing stopped them. They would disappear into the woods for hours every day with refreshment breaks at the house of Gramps and Granny, who lived next door.

Gramps would call out from the garden, where he was hoeing his sweet corn, "You boys been working on Deep Pond? How deep is it now?" Granny would take a break from picking strawberries and quickly fix them pizza and Pepsi. The grandsons always received a warm welcome there.

Getting the dam to hold was a difficult proposition. Each day when they went down, water would be trickling through their dam of trees, stones, twigs, and mud.

John suggested, "Let's add some leaves to the mud and twigs." While that perhaps doesn't seem like a great idea...it worked! The dam held! After three hard weeks of work, the boys stood back and viewed their finished project.

Crystal clear water spilled over the rock ledge until it tumbled into the stream below. The boys would strip down to their shorts and get in their pool almost every day. The water was four and a half feet deep, so they named their new creation, Deep Pond.

"John, let's be very quiet and see what animals come to get a drink from the pond." The boys sat on the bank and watched as squirrels, rabbits, and a deer came to sip from the cool, refreshing water.

"Yikes! There's a snake!" But it slithered on past to get to the rocks warmed by the sun. Once in a while even a fox moved gracefully through the woods to take a sip of water downstream. Tadpoles swished through the water while frogs croaked from the bank. A varied ecosystem awaited them each day.

This project always needed attention. Nearly every day they spent a half hour or so reinforcing the dam with more mud, leaves and twigs. They wanted it to last as long as possible.

These two young engineers took pride in their accomplishment. When friends visited, their eyes lit up in wonder at Deep Pond. Some thought it too cold for a swim, but all enjoyed exploring the nearby woods and gathering berries for a refreshing snack.

This was one of those times when the brothers worked well together. Time for fighting didn't exist, as they had an idea and wanted it to succeed. Just like that other time when they worked diligently in the middle of the corn field to build a bomb shelter in the ground. They dug so deep they had to use a ladder to get in and out. Television told about the dangers of tornadoes and nuclear bombs so the boys wanted the family to be prepared. Working together made projects easier.

Using their creative minds during summer break certainly taught them more than sitting all day watching television or playing video games. Their sharp minds learned to create new ideas, which in turn would help them with schoolwork and life for years to come.

The pond walls didn't hold through the winter weather and spring rains. The boys didn't try to build it again. They had succeeded in creating Deep Pond and would always have fond memories of their time working together and enjoying a cool swim on a hot day.

Wish someone had thought to take a picture!

Ugly duckling

A young man was waterskiing when he fell into the river. As the boat circled to pick him up, he noticed a hunter sitting in a duck boat in the reeds. The water skier raised his hands in the air and joked, "Don't shoot!"

The hunter responded, "Don't quack."

Over your head?

Never test the depth of the water with both feet.

What Am I?

BY HARRIETTE MCBRIDE ORR

Betcha can't guess.

 The 1600s saw my Birth, so I have been around forever, it seems.

Early on, I was just a convenience but, by the 19th century, I became a necessity of detailed and ornate design. In some cases, really a work of art, depicting fashionable ladies and pastoral scenes. My favorites were the racy pinup girls of the time.

You may find me in all shapes and sizes. Sometimes I am round and made from glass; often made of pottery or brass. I tend to come in an array of colors.

My prices range from very cheap to high dollar.

Stands are made for me to rest upon, or I sit flat upon the table.

Some of my bottoms are cloth, like a beanbag.

To a mother's horror, babies love to stir in me and spill my contents down their fronts.

Alas, my time has come and gone. No longer in style, I am banned from most places. Most people do not smoke anymore, so they have no need to know "who burned the hole in the tablecloth."

Now do you know what I am?

UNBELIEVABLE

un•be•liev•a•ble (ŭn'bĭ-lē'v'ə-bəl) *adj.* too improbable for belief; of such a superlative degree as to be hard to believe. **—un•be•liev•a•bly** (-blē) *adv. Syn:* beyond or past belief, incredible, inconceivable, staggering, unimaginable, not to be credited, dubious, doubtful, improbable, questionable, implausible, palpably false, unveracious, open to doubt, a bit thick.

Desert Dream
Based on a True Story

BY BEVERLY WENCEK KERR

A story of sand and savvy on the trail

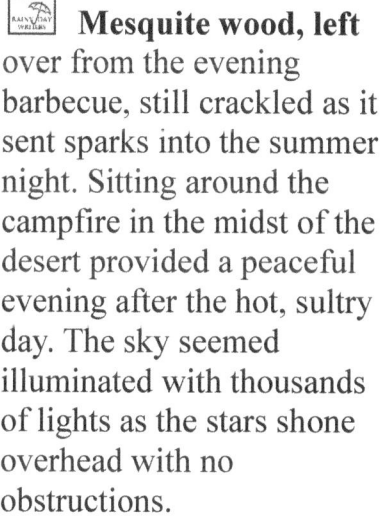 **Mesquite wood, left** over from the evening barbecue, still crackled as it sent sparks into the summer night. Sitting around the campfire in the midst of the desert provided a peaceful evening after the hot, sultry day. The sky seemed illuminated with thousands of lights as the stars shone overhead with no obstructions.

It was quiet here too. The only sound was an occasional cry of a coyote or a roadrunner's call. With a refreshing cup of prickly pear tea in hand, Lydia relaxed while watching the firelight flicker against the arms of the saguaro. This seemed quite the change from camping out at Seneca Lake when she was home in Ohio, but Lydia had left home several months ago for a gypsy trip throughout the United States.

For the last few weeks, she had been camping in the desert of Arizona. Some friends from Ohio lived there and helped guide her to exciting places for exploration. One of those old friends, Jake, had become a rancher and promised to take her on an exciting ride the next day. Jake had been a long-time friend and neighbor of her family back in Ohio, so she knew he was trustworthy.

Even though the daytime temperatures reached over a hundred degrees, nights in the desert usually cooled down for a good night's sleep. Lydia closed the camper door to ensure that no desert creatures joined her during the night. She drifted off to sleep thinking about her promised ride through the desert in the morning.

All at once, Lydia sat up in bed, shaking all over. *That was a terrible dream!* She jumped out of bed and, as soon as her feet hit the floor, the details of the dream were forgotten. This often happened to her if she didn't write down her dream while still in bed. But since she was still shaking, she tried to recall what had scared her so drastically.

Before long, Jake honked the horn outside the camper. "Come in for a cup of coffee," shouted Lydia. "We have all day to explore the desert."

"But we can't dally too long or it'll get blazin' hot," Jake remarked as he hopped out of his pickup truck with his dog, Dusty, close behind.

It didn't take long for Lydia and Jake to drink a cup of coffee and sample some fresh muffins Lydia had baked before the sun heated up her small camper.

"Where do ya wanna go today?" Jake questioned.

"I've never been up in the mountains on the other side of Crystal Creek. Someone said they once had a gold mine up there. It might be fun to explore."

"Well, we can explore if you want," Jake grinned, "but don't get your heart set on findin' any gold. It was probably only fool's gold anyway."

Off they headed, through the desert and into the mountains. While Lydia enjoyed the desert scenery, which was nothing like Ohio, the mountains made her smile. Even in July, the tops were covered in snow and there were pine trees up here instead of cactus. Hard to imagine the heat of the desert below and snow still existing on the peaks of the mountains.

Jake enjoyed showing his friend the territory and suggested they take a back road, which just might lead to an old gold mine. Of course, Lydia bounced in her seat with excitement. She loved to explore the back country!

The highway soon turned into a dirt road running along the edge of the mountain. The higher they drove, the narrower the road seemed to become. All at once Lydia shouted, "Stop!"

Jake just smiled with confidence as this was his territory. "It'll be okay. I know how to drive these roads."

"No, Jake, I'm serious, you have to stop." By now, Lydia was shaking from head to toe, and her skin had turned as white as the clouds in the sky.

Jake pulled the truck over to the edge of the road once he saw how pale Lydia looked. "What's the problem, Lydia. What's spooked ya?"

"Oh, Jake, now I remember my dream last night. In my dream, I was riding in a truck along a mountain road and, just around a bend, the road disappeared. It had fallen away completely. The truck was going over the edge when I woke up."

"Now, Lydia, there'd be a sign if there was a problem with the road. You don't know this country like I do."

But Lydia would not take no for an answer. "You walk around that bend up there before we drive any farther, and see if it's okay."

Jake put his cowboy hat on and reluctantly walked up the road as Lydia requested. He shook his head as he muttered, "Women!"

Lydia sat inside the truck anxiously awaiting Jake's report. She hoped she was wrong, but something deep inside her, call it woman's intuition if you will, told her a problem existed up ahead.

It didn't take long for Jake to return with a look of disbelief on his face. "The road's all washed out. Must'a been from that storm a couple days ago. No one comes up this way very often. How'd you know that?"

"I told you. I had a dream." She pulled her serape tight around her even though it was a summer day.

Jake motioned to Lydia, "Walk with me around the

bend and see the road, or what used to be a road."

"No thanks," Lydia shivered. "I already saw it once during the night. You need to listen to your dreams when you remember them. Sometimes they're given to us for a reason. This time it saved our lives...and your truck."

That road trip would not soon be forgotten. Lydia's angels were busy at work again.

Now, that's tough

Three cowboys sat around a campfire out on a lonesome Texas prairie, each with the bravado for which cowboys are famous. A night of tall tales begins.

The first one starts, "I must be the meanest, toughest cowboy there is. Why, just the other day a bull got loose in the corral and gored six men before I wrestled it to the ground by the horns with my bare hands."

The second cowboy won't be bested. "Why, that's nothing! I was walking down the trail yesterday and a fifteen-foot rattlesnake slid out from the brush, coming straight toward me. I grabbed that snake with my bare hands, bit off his head, and sucked the poison down in one gulp. And I'm still here today."

The third cowboy remained silent, silently stirring the coals with his hands.

I Never Believed in Ghosts

BY DONNA J. LAKE SHAFER

In the spirit of enduring love.

I never believed in ghosts...until last night.

My wife, Sarah, died in a car accident two years ago. We had been high school sweethearts and had been madly in love. We knew our love would last forever.

Only recently Sarah's personal belonging as well as mementos of our life together were packed away.

A few months ago, a new associate was hired at our firm. Her name is Maggie and we have been working together on a particular case. We have become good friends, but I've been reluctant to ask her out because of...what? Guilt, I suppose.

Yesterday, after work, I returned home and there on the foyer table was a single item—the heart-shaped necklace I gave Sarah on our first wedding anniversary. How could this be, I asked myself. It had been locked in her jewelry box when it was stored away. Picking it up, I felt rather than heard Sarah's voice, saying that she would always love me and knew that I would always love the memory of her. She was gone, but wanted me to be happy.

I read the engraving on the back of the necklace, "Forever." Holding it close for a moment, I kissed it, then slipped it into my pocket, until tomorrow when I will give it to our daughter.

And tonight, I will call Maggie and extend an invitation for dinner and a movie.

I can just taste it...

There was an elderly man at home, upstairs, dying in bed. He smelled the aroma of his favorite chocolate chip cookies baking. He wanted one last cookie before he died, so he dragged himself to the hallway, rolled down the stairs, and crawled into the kitchen, where his wife was busily baking cookies.

With his last remaining strength, he moved slowly to the table and was just barely able to lift his withered arm to the cookie sheet. As he grasped a warm, moist chocolate chip cookie, his favorite kind, his wife suddenly whacked his hand with a spatula.

Gasping for breath, he asked her, "Why did you do that?"

"Those are for the funeral."

Last Dance

BY MARTHA F. JAMAIL

An unexpectedly beautiful ending to an evening with friends.

Tucked into a quiet street in Sarasota, Florida, is a restaurant with a piano bar that provides live music every Friday night. Our friends had decided we should go there because of all the praise they had heard about the new chef. The live music would just be an extra we could tolerate because it was a piano and would not stifle our friends, who loved to converse over dinner.

When we arrived, Ed told the hostess we wanted a table for six and indicated a table on the restaurant side. The hostess said, "Since it's still early, I can seat the six of you in the piano bar. I think you'll really enjoy it there because Harry is coming tonight."

Ed laughed, "Well we don't really know who Harry is, and we want to have table conversation."

"Trust me, sir," insisted the hostess, "the music is not intrusive and you will enjoy Harry. He's a professional dancer, but you will have to stay for the last song in order to see him."

Ed looked at us and we all agreed to the piano bar. When our dinners arrived, the pianist began to play. The music was lovely and allowed for easy table conversation. The man at the piano was very gracious and said he would take requests, but the last request would be for Harry. The dance floor in the piano bar was no more than 10 square feet, but some couples did get up to dance.

The food was delicious and as we enjoyed the last of our dessert, an elderly gentleman walked in, carrying an old-fashioned mop. The kind of mop you have to wring out in a bucket. He was dressed in a dark pin-striped suit, with a bow tie, and his hair, thin and white, formed a halo around his head. He walked slowly to the man at the piano, whispered something to him, and placed some bills in the request jar.

There was muted laughter when everyone saw the mop, not knowing what to expect, but soon the music started, a beautiful, haunting melody…perfect for a slow dance. As the man moved around the dance floor, he held the mop head tenderly against his arm, and supported the stick on the top of his shoe. With each graceful movement and twirl, the strands on the mop swayed as if they were a woman's hair. As he danced he looked at the mop with such tenderness, you could almost see the lady in his arms. There was no doubt he was a professional dancer and, when the music ended, he lowered the mop into a final dip.

The entire restaurant cheered and gave him a standing ovation. There were tears in my eyes, because I just knew the phantom lady he was dancing with was someone he truly cared for.

On our way out, the hostess caught my eye and I couldn't resist going over to ask her about Harry's dance partner. She said that Harry and his wife often came there to dance, and since she had passed away he honored her memory by coming there and dancing to their favorite song.

The Ghost of Joe Vargo

BY SAMUEL D. BESKET

At first it sounded like a gentle rattle, a rustling of leaves against a window pane, then it grew louder.

Prologue

From the moment Joe laid eyes on Anna, he knew he would marry her someday. How he would accomplish this he didn't know, since all he knew was her name and that she had emigrated from Czechoslovakia the same year he did, in 1910.

Anna's transition into American society was easier than Joe's. She finished high school and had a good paying job at Universal Potteries in Cambridge.

Joe was the opposite. His uncle got him a job at the Webster Coal Mine, east of Senecaville. When he wasn't working at the mine, he spent his spare time playing cards and drinking. Then one day at a Holy Name Society picnic, he asked her to dance. It was love at first sight. Exactly one year to the day, they were married in St. Andrew's Byzantine Catholic Church. It was the happiest day of Joe's life. Now, five years later, they had twin boys and were saving money for a small farm overlooking Leatherwood Creek, just south of Lore City.

 **Sleep came hard for Joe** that night. After tossing and turning for a few hours, he finally drifted off. The ringing of the alarm jolted him from his slumber.

"I wish you didn't have to work today," Anna said as

she rolled close to him. "Is everyone working?"

"No," Joe said as he stretched. "Just ten of us, we're going to shore up the roof in an old entry. The coal is high, almost six feet, but the slate is loose. I can make good money in that entry once we fix the roof."

"I wish you could stay home with us. The boys have Catechism. Remember, they make their first Holy Communion at Easter."

"I know," Joe said as he got out of bed. "We already told the straw boss we were taking three days off for Easter."

"I'll fix your breakfast," Anna said, kicking off the covers.

"Stay in bed," Joe said, as he threw the covers over her head. "You need the rest. All the guys are having breakfast at Mary's Restaurant."

Anna was more than happy to go back to sleep. Saturday was the only day she could sleep in.

The blast from the mine whistle echoed down the valley. Startled by the sound, Anna jumped out of bed. It could mean only one thing. There was an accident at the mine. Anna dressed quickly, called her neighbor to watch the boys, and started out the door. When she opened the door, she froze. Father Evanik was slowly walking across the yard. The look on his face and the vestments around his neck confirmed all her fears. Slowly, she sank to the floor, sobbing as she pulled her babushka over her head.

The next week passed in a blur. The house was full of friends and family. Then came the funeral and just as fast as they came everyone was gone, and she and the boys were alone.

All the beauty of Anna's world ended in that mine last week. The dream of raising a family with Joe was gone, buried under a ton of slate. It takes a special kind of courage to raise a family alone. Now she was faced with raising the boys on her own. Alone with her thoughts and fears, the days were hard, but the nights were brutal. *How do you shut off the mind*, she thought? Oh! How she dreaded being alone in that house at night.

Night after night, Anna tossed and turned, unable to sleep. Finally, out of desperation, she took some of Joe's clothes and laid them beside her in the bed. Exhaustion took over and she drifted off into a restless sleep.

At first it sounded like a gentle rattle, a rustling of leaves against a window pane, then it grew louder.

The boys forgot to put the cat out, was her first thought.

Rushing downstairs, Anna was surprised to see their cat, Gabriel, curled up in a corner on the back porch.

Must be dreaming, she thought as she went back upstairs to bed.

The next day passed quickly, Anna never gave the strange noise another thought. That night after putting the boys to bed, she readied herself for bed. Oh, how she hated the nights.

Once again, around one a.m., it started. Just a gentle rattle that slowly grew louder. Jumping out of bed, she raced to the kitchen. All was quiet and in order. Slowly, she made her way back up the stairs and fell into bed. After a week of sleepless nights, she had enough. *Tomorrow I will talk to Father Evanik; I can't keep going on like this.*

The church was packed that Palm Sunday morning. After returning to the rectory, Father Evanik had just poured himself a cup of coffee when he saw Anna standing at the door. Reaching for another cup, he motioned for her to come in.

"I have a ghost," Anna blurted out.

"A ghost!"

"Yes, a ghost, Father. It's rattling the pans in my cupboard."

"I don't believe in ghosts, Anna. Only the Holy Ghost."

"But, Father, I can't get any sleep. Something keeps waking me up."

"Well," Father Evanik said, looking at the calendar on the wall, "if it's a ghost, we can pray it out of there. How about Monday evening around six?" Anna nodded her head, drained her cup, and walked out the door.

Monday night came and Father Evanik arrived with several parishioners in tow.

"Now where do you think this ghost is?" he asked.

"In the corner cabinet, by the stove. It has some pans and Joe's tobacco tins."

"My, my," Father said as he looked at the tins of tobacco. "Cutty Pipe, that's pretty strong tobacco. Are all these full?"

"I don't know, Father. I can't bring myself to touch them."

One by one, he began picking up the tins and shaking them. The last tin, nestled in the corner, was quite heavy. As he set it on the kitchen table, he removed the top.

"Well, well," he said, "I think I found your ghost."

Anna walked over to the table and looked inside. Startled, she gasped and put her hand over her mouth.

"Are those silver dollars?" she asked.

"Yes, about a half-gallon of them. I don't think you had a ghost, Anna. I believe you were visited by an angel."

Later that night as Anna crawled into bed, her thoughts were on Joe. She was asleep in minutes, only to be awakened the next morning by two boys bouncing on her bed, screaming. "Mommy, Mommy, we're hungry."

Where the Magic Is

BY JOY L. WILBERT ERSKINE

Using your powers for good.

Three magical powers. That's all I want. Kind of like the mythical genie in the bottle who grants three wishes. I'd ask for magic powers of my own.

From my earliest recollection, I've always wished I could clean a house instantaneously from top to bottom and make it and everything in it brand new, spotless, and bug- and germ-free with a blink of my eyes. Cleanliness is a valuable commodity, but cleaning is a bothersome chore. It wastes so much time and it doesn't last. You can work all day at it and, next morning, *POOF!*—it's already starting to get dirty again. That's crazy! So my first magical power choice, since cleaning can't be once and done, is the next best thing—the ability to make everything spic and span and in good repair from cellar to attic with a snap of my fingers. Imagine how popular I'd be if I could do that everywhere I went!

Along those same lines, my second magical power would be to be able to "erase" things—like cigarettes and drugs from people's bodies, trash and litter from the streets, and bars and other adult businesses from the face of the earth, as if they'd never been there—simply by thinking it done. Whether traveling through town or across country, seeing things like these always sets my wisher wishing I could eliminate the bad stuff by just concentrating on it and "erasing" it from the picture. Life would be more pleasant and productive without the negative influences and dirty situations we see every day.

Magical power #3 would be the best of all. I'd like to be able to move mountains, not literally, but to see into people's hearts, understand their needs, and help them to feel hope and change their lives for the better. So many around us need to feel good about themselves again and don't know how to go about it. Hope changes people, and I believe hopeful people can change the world. Life isn't always easy, but an optimistic attitude is a real game-changer. And if hope comes from the heart, it transforms how we see ourselves and changes the horizons around us—it can move those mountains. That gives us what we all need—a better perspective.

Unfortunately, magic powers like these are pretty hard to come by. I may never be able to wave a sparkle wand at my house and have it clean itself, make bad habits disappear with a willful snap of my fingers or, like pulling a rabbit out of a hat, bring out the good in myself, let alone anyone else. But in my own little corner of the world, I still try to do my best. That's probably miracle enough. I've learned you don't have to be a wizard to cast a spell, if you have real magic in your heart.

ALL THE ANSWERS

ANSWERS to "Test Yourself" on page 36: 1c, 2a, 3b, 4c, 5a, 6d, 7a, 8d, 9b, 10c, 11c, 12d, 13d, 14c, 15b, 16a, 17a, 18c, 19c.

ANSWER to "Helpful Hardware Man" on page 93: House numbers 5-0-0-0.

RDW Sudoku — Level #1 Answer

H	C	E	D	G	B	A	I	F
A	I	D	H	F	C	B	E	G
F	B	G	A	E	I	C	D	H
C	G	F	B	H	D	E	A	I
E	A	B	I	C	G	H	F	D
D	H	I	F	A	E	G	C	B
G	F	A	C	D	H	I	B	E
B	E	C	G	I	F	D	H	A
I	D	H	E	B	A	F	G	C

RDW Sudoku — Level #2 Answer

D	I	A	C	H	F	G	E	B
E	B	F	G	A	D	I	H	C
G	C	H	E	I	B	F	A	D
I	D	G	H	C	E	B	F	A
H	A	C	B	F	I	D	G	E
F	E	B	A	D	G	C	I	H
A	H	I	D	G	C	E	B	F
C	G	E	F	B	A	H	D	I
B	F	D	I	E	H	A	C	G

RDW Sudoku — Level #3 Answer

F	B	E	D	A	C	H	I	G
A	G	D	I	H	E	C	F	B
I	H	C	G	F	B	A	E	D
G	A	H	C	E	D	I	B	F
D	C	F	B	I	A	E	G	H
B	E	I	H	G	F	D	C	A
H	I	B	E	D	G	F	A	C
E	F	G	A	C	H	B	D	I
C	D	A	F	B	I	G	H	E

RDW Sudoku — Level #4 Answer

F	I	C	G	E	A	H	B	D
H	B	G	F	C	D	E	I	A
E	A	D	I	H	B	G	C	F
A	D	B	E	G	C	I	F	H
C	E	I	A	F	H	D	G	B
G	H	F	D	B	I	C	A	E
I	F	E	B	D	G	A	H	C
D	G	H	C	A	F	B	E	I
B	C	A	H	I	E	F	D	G

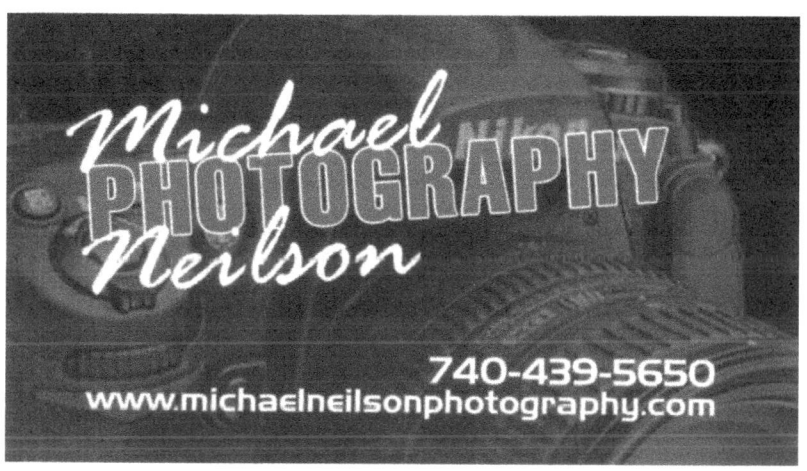

Mike Neilson is the official photographer of the Rainy Day Writers. Mike's photography website is just a click away using the QR code below, or find him at www.michaelneilsonphotography.com for award-winning photography.